"The cake, Abby, the cake!"

Lady Jeffrey's excitement alarmed Abby so that she bade her sit down.

"Now, Aunt Bea," she said calmly. "What about the cake?"

Lady Jeffrey snatched Abby's hand and looked at her as if what she was about to disclose would be fit only for the Prince Regent's ear.

"My lemon cake, Abby," she said in a whisper. "It is a love potion, dear."

Abby rubbed her forehead and wished she had stayed abed as her first inclination had told her to do.

"Aunt," she said cautiously, "you didn't...surely you didn't say anything to anyone about your belief that the cake is magical?"

"Why, Abigail Milhouse!" Lady Jeffrey said, obviously much offended. "Why ever should I not? Just because you don't believe in my lemon cake doesn't mean..."

"Aunt Bea," Abby told her desperately. "You haven't thought. If the ton hears about your lemon cake, half of them will beat a track to the door hoping to discover your recipe, and the other half will dismiss us as bedlamites. We shall be ruined either way!"

THE LEMON CAKE

JUDITH STAFFORD

Harlequin Books

TORONTO • NEW YORK • LONDON
AMSTERDAM • PARIS • SYDNEY • HAMBURG
STOCKHOLM • ATHENS • TOKYO • MILAN

To Alfie Thompson,
whose friendship is truly magical

Originally published August 1990
Second edition October 1990

ISBN 0-373-31132-X

CHAPTER ONE

"Abby, I hear a carriage!"

"Don't be silly, Jonathan dear. No one would call on such a miserable afternoon."

"It's been snowing forever!" a beautiful young woman complained, her mouth drooping.

Abigail Milhouse, her older sister, only smiled at such an exaggeration, but a young woman who industriously stitched the hem of an embroidered handkerchief said, "No, Phoebe, only since yesterday."

"I know, I know, Mary, but it *seems* a long time. We had to miss the assembly ball, and it would have been our first since we've been out of black gloves."

A silence fell as each remembered the cause of their mourning: the death of their mother. It was broken by a rap on the sitting-room door followed by the entrance of their long-time butler, Austin.

"Miss Abby, Lady Jeffrey is here!"

"What? Here? But...how—how wonderful. Tell Mrs. Austin to prepare the yellow bedchamber," Abby ordered as she thrust aside her needlework and hurried to the door.

"Who is Lady Jeffrey?" Phoebe enquired in the wake of her sister's disappearance.

"Isn't she Papa's sister?" Mary asked.

Jonathan, only four when his father had died suddenly in a hunting accident four years before, asked, "Who?"

"I think..." Mary stopped as the door reopened to reveal their sister, accompanied by a rounded female form which only reached Abby's shoulder. Little else was visible, due to the numerous scarves in which the lady was swathed.

"Come close to the fire, ma'am. You must be frozen, travelling in such weather."

"Nay, child, I'm used to the cold," the mummified figure said in muffled tones even as she drew near the roaring fire. The young people fell back to give way to their guest. Abby assisted the woman in unwinding the several shawls that covered her head.

After she had been divested of her outer garments, Lady Jeffrey surveyed the occupants of the room. "Well, who have we here?"

"Oh, I'm sorry, Aunt Beatrice. Here is Phoebe—" Abby paused as the young woman gave a creditable curtsy "—Mary—" who followed her sister's example "—and Jonathan, who was only a baby when...when you were here for Papa's funeral."

"Ah, yes, a sad occasion. Come here, Jonathan."

The young boy walked over to the guest and stood patiently while she searched in her reticule for a pair of eyeglasses which she pushed onto her small nose. "Oh, my, yes. He does have the look of dear George, doesn't he? How he takes me back to my childhood," she said, as she patted his cheek.

Jonathan squirmed in silent protest beneath his sister's stern eye. He considered himself much too old for such babyish treatment.

The guest turned her attention to the young ladies and nodded with a satisfied air before she raised a gloved finger and pointed at each of them. "Isn't there another one of you?" she queried with a puzzled look.

"Why, yes, ma'am. Kitty is doing her studies in the schoolroom."

"She is a bluestocking?" the woman asked in horror.

There were muffled giggles from three of the young people followed by a stern look from Abby. "No, ma'am, not at all," she answered. "Kitty is there as punishment for misbehaviour."

"Ah . . . well, as long as she's not bookish."

"Mary's the one who likes books," Jonathan said.

That young lady blushed and looked beseechingly at her older sister.

"That will do, Jonathan, or you will find yourself in attendance upon Kitty." That settled, Abby turned to defend Mary. "Mary is fond of reading, ma'am, but no more than others."

Mary squirmed under the intense examination their guest directed at her. "She's pretty enough to be forgiven, perhaps, though, of course, she don't hold a candle to this one."

Phoebe, the recipient of such a handsome compliment, protested, "Mary is very pretty, and much cleverer than I!"

"That's what I said, girl," Lady Jeffrey agreed.

A change of subject was called for, and Abby said, "We are delighted you have come to visit us, Aunt Beatrice. After such a long journey, I hope you intend to stay for a while."

"Why, my dear—" the lady blinked in surprise "—I've come to take you all to London. Didn't you receive my letter?"

There was a startled silence before Abby said faintly, "No, ma'am, we did not."

"No? What could have become of it? I gave it to Jackson . . . no, no, I put it in my knitting bag. My, I do believe I left it there. Yes, that's where it is."

"Just . . . just what did your letter say?" Abby asked.

"Why, that I'm taking you all to London to find husbands, of course."

Abby fell silent. It was Mary who voiced a protest.

"But there are four of us, Aunt Beatrice."

"Well, of course there are. I counted you, didn't I? And there was one missing, the bookish one, wasn't it?"

Mary didn't attempt to correct the lady's misconception, but turned questioning eyes to Abby.

Jonathan considered contributing to his aunt's idea of his sisters, but Abby's earlier admonition held him back.

"Ma'am, I admit I have been considering the need to present Phoebe and Mary, but I have not yet decided—"

"Phoebe and Mary? Just two? No, no, we must have all of you at once. Waste of time to have to go again next year."

"But Aunt Bea, I am beyond the age of marriage and even with only three to present, there is no surety that all three girls will discover a . . . will find an acceptable match."

"O'course they will. And you, too, miss! Too old! Ha! Anyway, I have a secret which will ensure our success."

Looks of curiosity, excitement and doubt were exchanged, but the three younger Milhouses left it to their sister to respond to their guest's amazing statement.

"I don't understand, ma'am."

"Well, and there's no reason why you should. Just never you mind. All you need to do is see to the packing. I've leased a house and reserved a date for our ball . . . and if George didn't leave you beforehand with the world, well, I'll see to your expenses. After all, I've no chicks of my own, so it will all come to you, anyway."

"That—that is very kind of you, ma'am, but there is no problem about funds. Papa provided for all of us, though, of course, we are not heiresses. But are you sure we can manage?"

"'Course we can manage. Better than that, we'll see all of you properly settled."

Silently pondering her aunt's reference to her "secret," Abby asked, "When were you thinking of going to London?"

"In the morning. No point in my unpacking here just to do it all over again."

"But, ma'am, we cannot...that is, there is much to be done before we could absent ourselves for a number of months from the estate. And we must pack."

"But what have you been doing since I wrote you? I thought you'd be all ready when I got here!"

"Aunt Beatrice, you forgot to mail the letter, remember?" Mary inserted, coming to aid of her stunned sister.

"What's that?"

Jonathan, fascinated by their guest, now moved back to her side and yelled, "You forgot to mail the letter."

"What's the boy yelling for? I'm not hard of hearing," Lady Jeffrey demanded of Abby while she stared through her spectacles at the young boy.

"But you didn't—" Jonathan tried to explain.

"Dear, why don't you go up to the schoolroom and ask Kitty to come make her curtsy to Aunt Beatrice."

"All right, Abby, but—"

"Now, please, Jonathan."

Though her words were crisply delivered, they were accompanied by a warm smile which relieved their sting. However, he didn't hesitate to obey her. Abby was fair but she required obedience.

Ignoring what had just transpired, Lady Jeffrey demanded, "Well, how long will it take to pack?"

Abby pulled her attention back to the diminutive lady. "Why...I suppose we could manage in a week or two, Aunt Beatrice, if...if we decide—"

"Decide? There's nothing to decide. This is what both your parents would want and that's what I'm here to do. Don't worry your head over it, girl. Just start packing."

Abby had run the household the past four years. Her mother had been bedridden for three of those years before dying. But if she resented someone else taking charge, it didn't show on her face. "I suppose you are right, Aunt Beatrice. Mama told me to—"

"Abby, Jonathan says you intend to go to London!" the fourth young lady of the Milhouse family said as she burst into the room.

"Kitty, make your curtsy to Aunt Beatrice and beg her pardon for your unladylike behaviour."

"But, Abby—"

"No, Kitty." The steel in her voice was not cloaked and her youngest sister followed her orders. Immediately upon rising from her curtsy and her apology, she swung back to her sister, a frown on her face. "Is it true, Abby?"

"Yes...yes, it is," Abby said, realizing for the first time that her mind was firmly made up.

"Well, I'm not going. I'll stay here and take care of the estate."

Abby sighed. That remark would have been laughable had it not foretold a stormy argument.

"Dear, I believe we can leave the estate in the trustworthy hands of Mr. Thompson."

"Besides, girl, you won't catch a husband here in the country," Lady Jeffrey inserted.

"But you are wrong, ma'am. I have already caught one . . . and he's the heir to an earldom."

"Kitty, there is no engagement, and even if there were, it would be vulgar to brag."

"But, Abby, you know Peter wants to marry me. It is only because you will not allow it that we are not married."

"Excuse us, Aunt Beatrice, for washing our dirty linen in your presence. May I show you to your room?" Abby asked.

Lady Jeffrey cut off Kitty's protest at being ignored. "Is what she says true?"

Abby hesitated before saying, "Yes, ma'am. I feel that Kitty is too young to become engaged. She just turned seventeen last week."

"Hmm, old enough in the eyes of the ton," Lady Jeffrey mused.

"See, Abby!" Kitty crowed.

"But I believe you are right," Lady Jeffrey continued, ignoring Kitty's protests. "Once she has been to London, learned to moderate her behaviour, she will be ready for marriage."

"No! No! I will not wait! You cannot do this to me!" Kitty protested.

"Kitty, go to your room at once."

Even in her anger Kitty knew when her sister had reached the end of her patience. With an anguished cry, she ran from the room.

"I apologize again, ma'am. She is not usually so . . . so volatile."

"It's the age. She'll outgrow it. But it would be wise to present her before allowing her to make her choice."

"Yes . . . well . . . there is so much to do I do not know where to begin."

"We can't linger here long. You two, I forget your names, go to your rooms and look through your wardrobes. Take only the most fashionable gowns. We'll buy new things in London, so there's no need to take anything out-of-date. And you, young man, go and find the house-keeper and desire her to wait upon us here."

The three younger Milhouses looked to their sister for confirmation of the orders. Abby smiled wryly and nodded, wondering if she was making the right decision. She wasn't even certain she had a choice in the wake of Aunt Beatrice's arrival.

Once the others had left the room, Abby posed the question that had been bothering her. "Aunt Beatrice, truly I am grateful for your assistance, but . . . but what is this secret you have mentioned?"

"Never you mind, Abigail. I'll reveal my secret at the appropriate time and not before."

"But Aunt Beatrice—"

"Nay, child, you'll not get it out of me. Now, best to make a list of things to be done. 'Course, I always lose my lists, but I feel much better for having made one. Fetch some paper."

A WEEK LATER, early in the morning, the members of the Milhouse household, plus Aunt Beatrice, entered the two carriages waiting in the cold winter air in front of their residence and embarked on the two-day trip to London.

Lady Jeffrey settled in amongst the robes and hot bricks as if she were a veteran traveller. Phoebe shivered, though she was heavily wrapped, her face troubled. Mary, the third member of their party, showed interest in the proceedings, never having travelled beyond their parish. Besides, she had a favourite book to while away the hours when the novelty wore off.

In the second carriage, Abby, after a tearful goodbye to Austin and his wife, was checking one of the long lists Aunt Beatrice had made and Abby had managed to keep up with. Tucked up beside her, Jonathan was already struggling from under the thick covers to press his face against the window. The third occupant in their carriage, Kitty, sat rigidly staring, determined to convey her protest with her body even if Abby would not allow her to speak.

After several miles, Abby said quietly, "You should relax, Kitty, or you will be quite sore. That would make tomorrow's ride most uncomfortable." Since she continued to study the papers in her hands and did not look at her youngest sister, Kitty permitted herself the slightest relaxation.

"But, Abby, you cannot know..." she began.

Holding up her hand to halt her sister's words, Abby said with a smile, "It would be impossible for me not to know, my dear. You have been at great pains to inform all of us the entire week."

"I know, but you have never experienced *Love*! That is why you are being so cruel!"

Abby gave no sign of the hurt her sister's remark gave her. It was true. She had never experienced that highly celebrated emotion, love. And was not likely to. At the advanced age of twenty-three, she had accepted her role in life as that of older sister, perhaps loving aunt, but never wife or mother. By the ton's reckoning, she had been on the shelf for a full three years at least.

When Abby did not respond to her sally, Kitty wondered if she had gone too far. "I'm sorry, Abby, if I have upset you, but Peter—"

"Peter is going to arrive in London shortly after you do, my dear, so you may save your complaints."

"What?" a stunned Kitty gasped, staring at her sister.

"I discussed the situation with Lord and Lady Abbott, and they decided it would not hurt Peter to receive a little Town bronze. We also decided not to inform the two of you of the treat in store for Peter until after our departure."

"Peter is coming to London!"

"Yes, but you must promise not to show him any particular favour for a while."

"Why?"

"Because if you appear to be engaged already, then the purpose of presenting you is lost."

"I think it is cruel to Peter to seek a better match."

Abby sighed. She was sick to death of these arguments on top of all the packing and preparations. "We are not trying for a better match. I only want you to be sure that you . . . that Peter is the person whom you wish to marry."

"But I have told you—"

"Yes, yes, yes. You have told me *ad nauseam*, child, but you have failed to convince me, because Peter is the only young gentleman of any rank with whom you have an acquaintance."

"I will still want to marry him, no matter how long you force me to stay in London."

"So be it. If, after a Season in London, he is your choice, you will not hear any objections from me."

IN THE LATE AFTERNOON of the second day, the carriages entered London, and, in spite of her tiredness from two days' travel with a small boy and a disagreeable young woman, Abby sat on the edge of her seat, leaning towards the window. She feared that Aunt Beatrice, no matter how kind she appeared to be, might have forgotten to lease the house. Or that, long absent from London, she might have chosen one in the wrong part of Town.

One might as well not come if the house was in Cheapside, or some other vulgar neighbourhood. And then there was the question of the staff. Austin had not wanted to leave the estate, but he had volunteered to accompany them because of the importance of their venture. But Aunt Beatrice had already hired the staff, sight unseen. It seemed the owner was abroad and had leased his staff as well as his house to Aunt Beatrice.

In spite of her youth, Abby felt responsible for her little family. Her mother had left her guardian of them, an unusual move, but one Abby desired. She did not want them to be divided among more distant relatives. Mary and Phoebe were not a problem, and even Jonathan, though sometimes he got into scrapes, was manageable. It was Kitty who disrupted the smooth fabric of their days. Now, with the strain of a London Season and all it entailed facing her, Abby was worried.

One of her worries was dissolved when the carriage stopped in front of a large mansion on a quiet, tree-lined square, in one of London's most elegant neighbourhoods. Now, if only Aunt Beatrice had actually remembered to lease it. A footman in forest-green livery appeared at the door of the carriage and swung it open. Abby took the hand he offered and stepped down. She saw Aunt Beatrice standing by the other carriage, awaiting Mary and Phoebe's descent.

At the top of the steps leading up to the massive front door stood an austere-looking butler. Aunt Beatrice motioned for Abby to accompany her, and the two of them moved up the stairs to meet him.

"You are Healy?" Aunt Beatrice demanded.

"Yes, Madam. You are Lady Jeffrey?"

"That's right. And this is my niece, Miss Milhouse."
She gestured to the others now coming up the stairs, "and
her brother and sisters."

They all trooped into the vestibule where a number of
servants were awaiting them. Healy presented Lady Jeffrey to each of the servants and she in turn introduced her
charges. Mrs. Healy was the housekeeper. Abby hid her
smile as the butler and his wife stood side by side. Healy
was tall and spare while Mrs. Healy was on the short side
and quite rounded. She greeted everyone kindly until
Jonathan appeared before her. Then her face split into a
wide smile. "Welcome to London, Master Jonathan."

Another of Abby's worries was removed, since the
woman appeared delighted to have a small boy in the
household. She took a moment to express her appreciation to the housekeeper, thereby winning that lady's approval for her thoughtfulness.

Healy interrupted their happy conversation with an
austere, "Tea will be served in the parlour, Lady Jeffrey,
if you wish."

"That will be lovely, Healy. Jonathan might prefer a
snack in the schoolroom, however."

"I think, Aunt Beatrice, just for this evening he would
like to be with us." Abby made her suggestion quietly. She
had allowed her aunt control over their withdrawing to
London, but she did not want her brother banished immediately upon their arrival.

"Of course, if that is what you prefer, Abigail. I simply
did not want him bored with female chatter."

"I think he can stand it for once. Right, Jonathan?"

The boy nodded his head, his eyes shining at his sister.
Even though he was normally adventurous, he was finding his new surroundings a bit overwhelming.

"Don't you worry, Miss Milhouse," Mrs. Healy whispered before going downstairs, "I'll send up some chocolate and a gingerbread man for the young master."

Both Abby and Jonathan felt better at her words, and everyone followed Healy into the parlour.

"Hmm, not bad," Lady Jeffrey said as she scanned the pleasant room. Abby, looking at the eggshell-blue walls, the two royal-blue damask sofas with tiny pink roses scattered at random, the elegant occasional tables, and several ornately carved chairs with seats covered in a pale rose velvet, felt her aunt could have been more approving.

Mary agreed with her. "Aunt Beatrice, this is the most elegant room I have ever seen! And look at this exquisite vase," she added, approaching a blue vase filled with pink roses.

"It's tolerable, Mary, but you know, the Egyptian style is all the rage now. This isn't really up-to-date."

Abby, seeing a frown quickly smoothed from the butler's imperturbable face, said, "We find it charming, Aunt Beatrice, and since we are only leasing, I think we are fortunate to find such a wonderful place."

"Perhaps we should think about redecorating, however. We wouldn't want anyone to think we were behind the times."

"Oh, no, Aunt Beatrice, please. I...I love this room. If the rest of the house is as charming as this, I shall never want to leave," Mary enthused. "Don't you think so, Phoebe?"

"Well, it is pleasant enough, but I wouldn't want to be thought unfashionable."

"I can assure you, Madam," Healy intervened, as if he could not be quiet another moment, "Lord Harrington has never been considered unfashionable."

"Who is Lord Harrington?" Jonathan asked, impatient for his tea but his attention caught by the new name.

"He is the owner of this establishment."

"Healy, why would anyone want to lease out such an elegant town home?" Abby asked quietly.

For the first time, Healy seemed unsure of himself. "I don't know, Miss Milhouse. His man of business assured the staff that this was his lordship's desire. He has been abroad for more than a year now."

"Doesn't he like England?" Kitty asked.

"Of course he does, Miss. Lord Harrington is the last descendant of a long and proud family. But he . . . sometimes he becomes restless."

"I would travel if I had the opportunity," Mary said softly, her eyes taking on a faraway look that was familiar to her family.

"Well, it is fortunate that he decided to do so," Lady Jeffrey proclaimed. "There were very few houses available this year and this one had by far the best location. When will that tea arrive, Healy? I am quite ready for it."

"I will see to it at once," Healy assured her, again the perfect servant.

When he had gone, Lady Jeffrey settled down on one of the sofas. "Well, we are here. Welcome to London, children. Now it is time to begin our campaign."

CHAPTER TWO

IN SPITE OF Abby's fears, Lady Jeffrey was a formidable campaigner. From friends with whom she had maintained a steadfast correspondence throughout her years in the north of England, she discovered the most favoured modiste of the fashion world for the coming Season and insisted that all four young ladies be fitted out "as fine as five pence."

Kitty protested at the amount of time involved in fittings when she had other things on her mind, and Phoebe, surprisingly to Abby, had little enthusiasm for her new clothes. It was Mary who delighted in their beauty and grew more confident in her new finery each day.

Of the four girls, Phoebe was clearly the most beautiful, her figure sure to have her acclaimed as a "pocket Venus." Her golden curls and limpid blue eyes were all the rage. Anything the dressmaker put on her only added glory to her beauty.

Kitty never regretted having darker blond hair because her vivacity caused eyes to be trained on her anyway. Her blue eyes were constantly sending out flirtatious looks which worried Abby, and her figure compared to Phoebe's, though she was slightly taller.

Tallest of all the sisters, Mary seemed a faded version of Kitty's vivacity and Phoebe's golden beauty. Her hair she termed a plain brown, ignoring its golden highlights, and her eyes were an icy blue that caused timorous young men to think twice before approaching her. In the country, her reputation for being quite knowledgeable added to the young men's fears. She had grown up thinking herself less than pretty and turned to books as her companions.

Mary had been Abby's greatest support and least source of worry during the past four years when she had raised the family alone and nursed their mother. Recognizing Mary's need for support now, Abby threw herself into making her sister feel more beautiful.

For herself, Abby accepted the clothes as necessary to accompany the girls as their guardian. But she too shared the Milhouse beauty. She thought nothing of her own pale blond hair, considering it dull next to Phoebe's golden locks, and her grey eyes, an inheritance from her father, only underlined her quiet air. She was almost as tall as Mary and understood her feeling of gaucheness when compared to her petite sisters. But Lady Jeffrey, looking at her four charges one afternoon several weeks after their arrival, saw a formidable array of beauty, one over which many mothers would gnash their teeth.

"Well, my dears, now that we are in form," she said, smoothing down the deep plum of her day dress, "it is time we begin our visits. I have made a list of those already in Town with whom I have an acquaintance. I shall expect at least one of you to hold yourself available every day for the next week or two to accompany me on these visits." All the while she was talking, Lady Jeffrey was searching her pockets, her knitting bag and the sofa upon which she was ensconced.

"What are you looking for, Aunt Bea?" Kitty demanded, distracted by her aunt's movements.

"My list. I had it not too long ago..."

"I have it in my room, Aunt Beatrice," Abby said. "You prepared it last week and I thought I would keep it until you needed it."

"Good girl. It is too bad you are to be married. You would be of such help to me when all this is over."

Abby smiled. "I am glad to hear it, Aunt Bea. It will be lonely for me once Jonathan is raised."

"Didn't you hear me, girl? I told you you would be married."

Abby only smiled wider and refused to rise to the bait. They had had several discussions over her future.

"Oh, Abby," Mary interrupted as she remembered something, "Mrs. Healy asked if she could speak with you. I forgot to tell you."

"Of course. I'll excuse myself for a moment, Aunt Bea." Abby left the room to seek out the housekeeper. After two weeks in the house, she had a great appreciation for the skills of Mrs. Healy and wanted to accommodate the woman in any way she could.

During her absence, Phoebe and Mary continued with their needlework and Kitty paced the room, complaining to whomever would listen that it had been more than two weeks since their arrival in London and she still had had no word from Peter.

"Faith, child, if the man loves you, he will call on you. If not, you are better off without him. It is important that the man have some feeling for you, at least at the beginning of the marriage, whether you do or not. That way it is easier to bend him to your will."

"Aunt Beatrice!" Mary protested, horrified.

The old lady smiled at her. "You will see, Mary. When a man believes himself in love with you, everyone is more comfortable because you have the ordering of his life. Men are relatively foolish creatures. They need a woman's guidance, but will not accept it except under the guise of romance."

In spite of Mary's reaction, Kitty found herself agreeing with her aunt. "It is true that Peter made a mess of things until I showed him how to go on. Now he and his father seldom argue."

Phoebe, her eyes anxious, said, "But I could not . . . I would not know how to . . ."

"It is all right, child," Lady Jeffrey said. "There is no need to be nervous. When one has your beauty, there is no need even to consider the man's needs. He will be anxious to care for you. All you must do is smile prettily and say thank you."

"Aunt Bea, I don't think—"

"Nay, Mary, it is only because you are young."

Abby's entrance brought a halt to the argument. She approached her aunt, sitting down beside her on the sofa. "Aunt Bea, Mrs. Healy told me you were in the kitchen this morning."

"Of course. A woman of Quality should always know what goes on in her own kitchens."

"Yes, but . . . it seems you upset Monsieur Pierre because . . . because you insisted upon baking."

"Man's a fool. Didn't think I would know what I was doing. Well, I showed him."

"But, Aunt Bea, why? If there was something you particularly wanted prepared, you only have to send the recipe to Monsieur Pierre. After all, we are paying him an excellent salary to prepare the very best meals."

"I know, but this was something special which I wanted to prepare for . . . for you."

Kitty, who had a sweet tooth, clapped her hands. "Oh, good! A treat. Are we having it for tea? What is it?"

"No...no, not today, child," Lady Jeffrey responded rather vaguely.

"But when? And what is it?"

"Kitty, do not badger Aunt Bea so," Abby remonstrated.

"It is only a lemon cake, Kitty," Lady Jeffrey responded, ignoring Abby's words. "But I want to save it for when we have guests."

"Lemon cake? I have never..." Kitty began, her mind on the proposed treat.

"Kitty, that is enough. It is very kind of you to go to so much trouble, Aunt Bea, but...next time, Monsieur Pierre would prefer that you give him the recipe. After all, once we are in the midst of the Season, you will not have the time to prepare such delicacies for us."

"Yes, well, we'll see," Lady Jeffrey mumbled vaguely as she began searching for something again.

Mary reached down and handed her her knitting bag, which had fallen to the floor. "Is this what you are looking for, Aunt Bea?"

"Yes, child, thank you. Such a sweet girl."

Abby sighed. She knew she would get no further reassurances from her aunt about remaining out of the kitchen. Mrs. Healy informed her that Monsieur Pierre threatened to leave at once if "that woman" ever dared to return to his domain.

"And it's not as if she turned out a masterpiece, Miss Abby," Mrs. Healy had said, having been on friendly terms with her new employer since quite early in their acquaintance. "Monsieur Pierre said it wasn't fitten to feed the pigs...and I must admit it didn't tempt my appetite."

And Aunt Beatrice wanted to save it for visitors. It seemed her warnings about the need for a good chef to entice their guests to return had nothing to do with her own efforts in the kitchen.

AFTER ANOTHER WEEK of visiting and being visited, the Milhouse household appeared settled in for the Season. The girls were pronounced prettily-behaved as well as beautiful and Lady Jeffrey was discovered to have a large acquaintance amongst the old guard of Society. Vouchers were obtained for Almack's, that venerable room where so many of Society's darlings sought the ultimate goal, an advantageous marriage.

While meeting the mothers and daughters of the Season, Lady Jeffrey had managed to snag introductions to a number of eligible young men, and on this day several arrived at the proper hour to call on the young ladies.

Abby greeted each of them with a warm smile, but she carefully studied them from under her lashes as she tried to determine their value as future husbands for her sisters. She felt uneasy in the role of parent on such an occasion, but there was no one else to take her place. Lady Jeffrey, while very helpful in launching her sisters, did not know them as Abby did. She felt each one required certain things in a husband.

Kitty needed a strong hand, she had decided early on, and Phoebe a very light one. And Mary—Mary required a loving one. How she was to find exactly what her sisters needed, she didn't know, but she was determined not to let anyone inappropriate near her beloved sisters.

She moved to the bell rope to ring for tea. Since their guests were only allowed to stay half an hour by Society's rules, there was no time to lose in showing off their superior chef. When several minutes had gone by and there was no answer, she whispered to Mary to determine what was keeping Healy. She herself had to remain in the drawing-room to keep a careful eye on Kitty.

Mary, nervous in the presence of the young gentlemen, gladly escaped from the room. She was crossing the hall to the butler's pantry when voices from the entrance below startled her.

"My Lord, we were not expecting you! How long... where have you... It is so good to see you, My Lord."

"And it is good to see you, Healy. I should have let you know I was coming, though everything seems to be in order. But I took a sudden urge to see England again. There was no point to sending a letter because it would have trailed my arrival."

Mary peeped over the bannister to see the butler standing next to an auburn-haired giant whose aura of dynamic energy bespoke a healthy man in his prime.

"Why do we have the town house open, Healy? Did my cousin require it? He is the only one I can think of who could command your services in my absence. Good old Giles. I have missed him. Has Thomas grown much in my absence?"

Mary had no idea who Thomas might be, but she recognized the young boy scooting past the two men without a look in their direction. Jonathan was halted however by a large hand. "Whoa, there, Thomas. Have you no greetings for your long lost cousin? Have I been gone so long that you do not recognize me?"

Mass confusion erupted as Jonathan protested with his hands and feet in a most painful manner at being halted in his tracks, and both Healy and Mary, descending rapidly from the first floor, tried to explain the identity of the boy.

Lord Richard Harrington, in spite of his travels among the heathens of the world, was a gentleman. With Mary's arrival upon the scene, he released the child and bowed, a look of surprise upon his face. "I beg your pardon, ma'am. I was unaware of my cousin's remarriage."

Mary, taken aback by this greeting, looked mutely at Healy.

"My lord, this is not...uh, permit me to introduce Miss Milhouse. She...that is, the Milhouses have leased your town house for the Season."

The identity of the man was thus explained to Mary, who had heard from the Healys of their employer in glowing terms, but Lord Harrington continued to stare at both the young lady and his butler.

Jonathan, who was collared by Mary as soon as Lord Harrington had released him, tugged on her sleeve. "Mary," he whispered, "I got to go to my room."

Mary nodded absently and released the boy, who sprinted up the stairs, distracting Lord Harrington from the other two. "That is not Thomas?" he asked.

"No, my lord, that is Mr. Jonathan Milhouse."

"I—I beg your pardon, Miss Milhouse," the tall man said, and Mary acknowledged his bow with a curtsy. She lifted her eyes back to his face as she rose. He was quite the most attractive man she had ever seen.

"Of course, sir. I daresay you are tired from your travels."

"Yes, but...did you say leased?" he demanded of his butler, dismissing Mary's words.

"Yes, my lord. Mr. Troutman, your man of business, assured us that was your intention. We were very pleased that he found such nice tenants," Healy added, smiling at Mary.

"But I left no such instructions!" Lord Harrington roared.

Both listeners were left speechless by his vehemence. "I will not have strangers in my house! How dare the man! He will not be my man of business when the sun sets! Clear the house of everyone, Healy. I shall return within the hour!"

By the time Mary and Healy recovered from Lord Harrington's outburst, he had disappeared out the front door, which was wrenched open by one of the footmen standing nearby.

"Healy, can he...? I know it is his house, but...but where will we go? There is nothing to be let at this late date. What shall we do?"

"There, there, Miss Mary. Not to worry. The Master has a temper, it's true, but he's always fair. Mayhap when he returns, he'll think again."

"So we must wait for his return? I do not want you and Mrs. Healy to lose your situations because you have not followed his directive."

"Bless you, Miss Mary. The Master wouldn't turn us off. Why, we've been working for him since he was a baby. You'll see. Just go back upstairs and wait. I'll have a word with him when he returns."

"Oh! That is why...I mean, Abby rang for tea, and...and when you didn't appear, she sent me to tell you that tea is...was required in the drawing-room."

"I'll see to it right away, Miss Mary, and send it up directly."

Mary composed herself and returned to the others, smiling at Abby's questioning glance. But inside, jumbled questions sought answers, and she could think of nothing but the tall man who held their fate in his hands. The visits seemed to go on forever, and she could not wait to tell Abby about what had happened.

LORD HARRINGTON STRODE from his Town residence in a towering rage. As a child, he had allowed his lamentable temper to get the better of him many a time, but a stern nanny and loving parents had taught him control. It was rare nowadays that he allowed himself the luxury of venting his anger.

But to return to his beloved home, ready to relax and enjoy the English spring, looking forward to greeting his servants, old friends of his childhood, and visiting with his only family, his cousin Giles, he had been overwhelmed by the outrage of having strangers invade his territory. By the time he had hailed a hackney cab and arrived at his solicitor's offices, he had regained control of his emotions. But in place of the fire that had burned in his green eyes, there was a coldness that would freeze the warmest heart.

Mr. Troutman, Lord Harrington's man of business for only the past three years, having inherited his business when his uncle passed away, had decided it was a shame that such a fine piece of real estate should go empty when he could lease it out and pocket the rental himself. After all, his client had gone out of the country and was not expected to return until the next Christmas, long after the Season had ended.

He realized his error the moment he looked up from his desk to see the powerful man bearing down upon him. There was no contest in either strength or right, and Mr. Troutman retired from the lists immediately. Grovelling and begging not to be sued, beaten, or murdered—any of the three seeming a probability in the face of his client's rage—he was greatly relieved only to be fired, with a demand for immediate settlement of all his lordship's accounts.

Lord Harrington named his cousin's man of business as the recipient of his finances and left the dingy offices before he lost control of his anger again. Once that had been accomplished, he re-entered the hackney coach and directed it back to his home. But as the cob drew the vehicle through the streets of London, he realized he still faced a most difficult problem.

In spite of his rage, he recognized the young lady, Miss...whatever her name was, was Quality. According to Mr. Troutman, the family who leased the house knew nothing of his scheme. Could he, a gentleman, turn them out? Legally, he had the right to do so, he believed, but to leave them homeless at the beginning of the Season, when nothing else would be available, would be an uncharitable thing to do. Well, he would request an audience with the man of the family, and perhaps something could be worked out.

His dismay when he discovered the man of the family was eight years old and had attempted to kick his shins at their last meeting, left him grasping for hope. He demanded of Healy who was in charge of the family.

"Well, Sir, there's Lady Jeffrey. She's the old lady, an aunt, it seems, and she's the one who leased the house, but it is Miss Abby who's in charge of the family."

"Miss Abby?" Lord Harrington demanded, his eyebrows raised at his starchy butler's familiarity with these strangers.

"Miss Milhouse, Sir. She's...well, the entire family is very nice, Lord Harrington. Miss Mary...she's the one you met earlier, she's most pleasant and helpful, too. She gave the tweeny some cream for a sore she had. And Miss Abby, she makes sure the servants aren't—"

"Healy! Please, I am having enough difficulty trying to throw these people out without hearing that they are paragons of virtue!"

Healy, hearing the plaintive tones that told him his master had recovered his temper, grinned at him. "I know, Master Richard, I mean, Lord Harrington. But it don't seem fair. Not that the missus and me don't want you back here. But these people came for the Season. And there's four of 'em to fire off, if you count Miss Abby, as I think you should, and—"

"All right, all right, I will not throw them into the street, but . . . but they are taking care of everything?"

Healy's grin grew. "Well, Lady Jeffrey did want to change the blue salon with Egyptian things, but Miss Abby and Miss Mary put a stop to that. Miss Abby said it wouldn't be right to do so since they were just staying for the Season, and Miss Mary, bless her, she just fell in love with that room."

"Ah, a lady of taste, I believe," Lord Harrington agreed, his face losing some of its tension. He had had the house redone just before his unexpected departure, thinking he was about to marry, but unforeseen events had changed his plans.

They were interrupted by Abby and Mary's emergence from the parlour. Mary had waited until the departure of their last guest, a late caller, before taking Abby aside and pouring her tale into her ear. Abby, relieved that Mary had shown the sense to keep it from their aunt and sisters, had immediately excused them both and come to talk to Healy.

"Ah, Miss Milhouse, may I present my employer, Lord Harrington," Healy swiftly said as the two young ladies descended the stairs. "And Miss Mary, whom you met earlier, My Lord."

Executing a perfect bow, Lord Harrington murmured, "Good afternoon, ladies."

Mary stared at this calm man. After his violent departure, she had expected him to return with a whip to drive them into the streets. Reading some of her thoughts, the gentleman smiled at her.

"I'm afraid I lost control at our earlier meeting, Miss Mary. I beg that you forgive my excessive anger and attribute it to exhaustion, as you so generously did earlier. I can promise it will not happen again."

Mary curtsied slightly in response to his speech, admiring his elegant demeanour.

"Lord Harrington, Mary has told me what has occurred. I feel there must be some mistake. Could we not discuss this . . . this problem with you?"

"Certainly, Miss Milhouse, I agree that there are several things we must discuss. If it is not too forward of me, may I suggest the library? We may be private there, and, again if it is not too bold of me, may I suggest Healy serve us tea? I find I am sharp set after my exertions."

"Of course, Lord Harrington. I pray you will forgive my lapse of hospitality. It is just that Mary's tale alarmed me. You see . . . we . . ."

"As I said, I was overly tired from my travels and did not, er, react in a manner becoming to a gentleman. I am sure we will come to an amicable agreement. Shall we?"

Abby and Mary preceded the man up the stairs to the library, wondering all the while whether they would have a roof over their heads by nightfall. Lord Harrington trailed in their wake, his eyes caressing his surroundings, homesickness adding to their considerable charms.

CHAPTER THREE

MR. GILES RUSSELL was descending from the schoolroom on the third floor, having visited with his son while the child ate supper, when he heard a familiar voice. He paused in surprise before hurrying down the stairs.

"Richard, you have returned!"

Lord Harrington looked up and greeted his cousin eagerly. "Giles! How good to see you. How are you?"

"I am fine, Richard. And you? We did not expect to see you before Christmas at the earliest."

"That's what my man of business thought, also," Lord Harrington said with a scowl.

Giles raised his eyebrows but vouchsafed no reply before he led his cousin into the library. Once the door was closed, he murmured, "A problem?"

"That fool leased out my house and pocketed the money, thinking I would never know."

Remnants of his anger still clung to his words, and Giles, the target of that same anger on occasion in the past, could not hold back a grin. "I assume you have confronted him with his sins?"

"Yes. And you may not be so amused when you discover his actions land me on your doorstep for the Season."

"Nonsense. You know Thomas and I will delight in your staying with us."

"Thanks, Giles. I suppose I should not have come home unexpectedly, but . . . I grew sick of foreign climes."

"And I should have kept watch on Troutman. I have heard rumbles of his dealings. I never even noticed your town house was occupied."

It was Lord Harrington's turn to grin at his cousin. "Of course you did not. You keep your nose too close to the grindstone. You will never be accused of being a social butterfly, coz."

Giles Russell grimaced at his cousin's words. He had caused consternation among the ton when he had become a businessman, spending his days operating a highly successful trading company as well as his three estates. And he did not even have the excuse of needing money. He was born of wealthy parents, an only son, and he had increased that wealth tenfold.

He moved to a small table and poured drinks for himself and his guest, handing a glass to Lord Harrington. He sipped the brandy before saying, "I would have lost my mind without my work to distract me, that and Thomas."

"I know, Giles, I know," Lord Harrington said, remembering that terrible time nine years ago when his cousin's wife had died in childbirth and his aunt's and uncle's deaths had followed in a terrible carriage accident as they rushed to comfort their son.

"Enough about me," Giles declared, "tell me about your travels."

For half an hour, Lord Harrington entertained his cousin with several of his more adventurous encounters with the Indians in America and the Maoris of Australia. Finally he called a halt to his reminiscences with a few questions of his own.

"How is Thomas?"

"Your nephew is growing taller every day. He's nine now, you know, and smart as a whip. His tutor must work to stay ahead of his student."

"I can't wait to see him. There's a small lad at my house whom I first took to be Thomas as he was dashing through the hall. But I soon discovered my error. He ruined the polish on my boots. Johnson will be furious with me."

"Johnson has remained with you?"

"Yes, though he swore the only reason he boarded the last ship was that it would bring him home to England. He's not a good sailor."

"You have been a sore trial to him."

Richard smiled. "That I have, but he has stood by me. As you have, Giles."

"What? I have not travelled with you to all those heathen places."

"No, but you always welcome me when I return."

"That's easily done. It is I who should be grateful that my celebrated cousin chooses to recognize an outcast."

"You still remain withdrawn?" Though the question was asked casually, Giles recognized the concern in his cousin's words.

"Never fear, Richard. It is by choice. While the ton detests my business affairs, they would gladly overlook them if I would only return to the fold and offer my wealth at the foot of some young miss with the proper bloodlines."

"But you will not do so."

"No, I will not. I cannot live my life in such a manner. I must be doing something. And I support hundreds with the jobs I have created with my company. Even if I wanted to become a man of leisure, I could not have those men on my conscience, many of them veterans of our war with France."

"Not to mention your many charities for those same veterans and their families."

Lord Harrington received only a frown in response. Giles Russell chose to hide his good works behind a cold façade. Richard smiled. "Well, you may find yourself forced to attend a few balls if you take me in, dear cousin. Would you do so for me?"

"I suppose so, but if you abandon me to any fortune-hunting Mamas, you will find yourself on the street. I will not be pursued every moment I am not safely in my own house. As it is now, I have complete freedom, and I do not want that to end."

"What about a Mama for Thomas?"

"Thomas is doing very well, thank you, without any unpredictable females in his life."

"And you still maintain a liaison with Mrs. Stevens?" Richard prodded with a grin.

"I do. It serves my needs without interfering with my life."

"Perhaps you are right. Certainly my last venture into romance played havoc with my life."

"But you must marry, Richard. You have the succession to think of."

"Thomas will succeed me, if I do not marry, so where is the problem?"

"I would not deny you the pleasure of your own son. Thomas is . . . is the most precious thing in my life. I wish you that joy also."

A crash interrupted their discussion and both men raced out into the hall where a gangly lad of nine years was picking himself up off the floor. Having heard of his uncle's arrival, Master Thomas had raced down to greet him and tripped on the last step. The prized blue vase on the side table had suffered greatly from his fall, and now lay on the floor in smithereens.

IT WAS NOT until after dinner that Giles Russell turned the subject back to his cousin's problems. "Who has leased your house? Anyone we know?"

"No, but they are a thoroughly decent lot. I could not bring myself to throw them out, although that was my first intention. Healy and his wife would never have spoken to me again if I had done so."

"Ah. They've taken to them, have they?"

"Yes. And it is no wonder. There is an old lady, Lady Jeffrey, and four beautiful young women, her nieces. Oh, yes, there is the young boy, Jonathan, I believe his name was."

"Lady Jeffrey? I do not remember that family."

"Well, as for that, the girls' name is Milhouse. They are all beauties."

"You mean they are firing off four in one Season? I have never heard anyone attempting anything of the sort."

"I wondered about it, also, but it seems their father died four years ago and the mother lingered for three years after his death, keeping to her bed. They have just come out of black gloves."

"And they confided all of this to you on your first visit?"

"No, of course not. We only exchanged the merest commonplaces once I had assured them I would allow the lease on the house to stand. It was Healy and his wife who told me all this. They have taken them under their wing, determined to help them have a successful Season."

"Are there no men in their family to guide them?"

"My very question when I first arrived back at the house. But Healy assured me the only man they had ever seen was Jonathan, the eight-year-old."

"Not exactly up to snuff at that age. Well, I daresay they will manage."

His cousin's casual dismissal of the ladies did not bode well for the plan that had germinated in Lord Harrington's mind since he had entered the parlour and met the other members of the household. While all the women were most attractive, Miss Phoebe was sure to be declared a diamond of the first water, and he thought she might even be able to draw his cousin back into Society.

"Probably, but I have offered my friendship to aid them. I promised to call on them on the morrow and hoped you would accompany me."

Giles sighed. "Richard, you know my days are filled with my business."

"It will not take long, Giles. And it would do you good. All work and no play, you know."

While Lord Harrington had always had a quick temper, he also had a charm that few could withstand. And in truth, Giles was lonely. He had few friends, by his own choice, and no social life. Lately he had found little joy in his days.

Perhaps Richard was right. He could spare the time to make a few social calls, attend a ball or two, without his business crashing down around his head. With a smile, he capitulated. "All right, Richard, I will accompany you, but I warn you. I cannot gad about like a frivolous dandy, so do not expect it of me."

"WELL!" Lady Jeffrey said after Lord Harrington's departure. "There goes a most eligible man. And Phoebe, I believe you caught his eye."

Mary's indrawn breath was overlooked by the family, for which she was grateful. She would not want anyone to know how attracted she was to the tall man. And if Phoebe had taken his eyes, her case was hopeless, anyway. She bent her head over her needlework.

Phoebe looked startled at her aunt's words. "But...but he did not speak to me, Aunt Bea."

"And what has that to say to anything, missy? Men don't marry for conversation."

"Our parents conversed constantly, Aunt Bea," Abby put in. "They were the best of friends."

"Well, they were the exception, my love. You cannot expect that kind of marriage in this day. Good bloodlines, health, pleasantness, and, of course, wealth, that's what you look for. And it appeared to me Lord Harrington had all those attributes."

Abby and Mary exchanged glances, but said nothing. Kitty, however, disagreed. "Peter and I converse. We will have a good marriage."

"You mean you tell Peter what to do and he does it," Mary said with a smile.

"Well, it's the same thing," Kitty assured her family. "Peter needs me!"

No one argued with her assessment, but it was the fact that Kitty controlled Peter that had led Abby to put off their engagement. Kitty unchecked might have disastrous results.

"Whether Lord Harrington was attracted to Phoebe or not," Abby said, "he promised to call on the morrow, and we certainly have cause to be grateful to him. I shudder to think what could have happened had he not been so generous."

"Where do you suppose he has been, Abby?" Mary asked, her curiosity getting the better of her resolve.

"I do not know, Mary, but perhaps even as far as America. It must have been a great distance."

"America! Oh, I have always longed . . ."

"Why would anyone want to go so far away?" Phoebe asked, puzzled.

"Oh, Phoebe, to see America! It is a huge country with giant forests and wide rivers. And the heathens there are called Indians and—"

"Mary, how you do go on. I would never leave the safety of England just to see some old trees."

With a sigh, Mary sank back into silence. Abby's sympathetic smile comforted her, but she knew Phoebe would never understand her desire to expand her horizons.

"The girl's right," Lady Jeffrey said. "I never want to go where I cannot be served a proper English tea."

"Well, fortunately, it is teatime, dear Aunt, so you may be assured of your proper English tea," Abby told her. "I must check on Jonathan before it is served. He has become restless, cooped up as he is here in the city."

ABBY SAT ALONE at the breakfast table the next morning, a frown on her forehead. She had not expected their stay in London to be free of problems, but several were giving her more concern than expected.

In the country, Jonathan had gotten into the normal scrapes of a small boy, but he had been happy. But after a month in London, his spirits were drooping. In spite of Abby's good intentions, there had been little time to spend with her brother. He moped around the big house, getting in the servants' way.

During the past week, she had interviewed several tutors, because she realized she would have even less time for Jonathan when the Season really began. Between dress fittings, chaperoning her sisters, returning social calls, holding open house herself and spending almost all of every night at social functions, she would not be able to give Jonathan the care he needed by herself.

But the interviews had been disheartening. She refused to tie Jonathan down to the shrewish, straitlaced men she had interviewed. One had even dared suggest she was incapable of interviewing him because she was a woman! With a sigh, she made a note to visit the employment agency again today to discover if there were any more candidates for the position.

Just as upsetting was the fact that she didn't think the girls were happy. Kitty was awaiting Peter's arrival and informing all and sundry of her discontent. And when the absent Peter did appear, Kitty would ignore all other men. The end result would be their engagement, which could have been achieved without the bother of a Season in London.

Phoebe, much to Abby's surprise, did not seem to be enjoying herself, either. Expected by everyone to be the most celebrated of the sisters because of her golden beauty, Phoebe had grown quieter. When the gentlemen had called this week, entranced with her fairy beauty, she had scarcely raised her eyes once.

Only Mary had really benefited from the move. Her tall figure was enhanced by her new clothes, which gave her an elegance she had heretofore not had. With it had come more confidence. In addition, the opportunity to visit museums, the lending library and even the Royal Zoo was a delight to Mary's enquiring mind. Jonathan, too, had enjoyed the Zoo, Abby remembered with a smile. So she could count Mary's happiness as a gain...unless she thought about last night.

For some reason, Mary had seemed subdued last evening. But Abby could not pinpoint any occurrence which had brought about Mary's withdrawal. With a sigh, she poured herself another cup of tea. If Mary was not going to be happy in London, either, they might as well go home and give the house back to Lord Harrington.

Her solitary ruminations were ended by her aunt's arrival. "Aha! Already up and about, are you? Once the Season begins in earnest, you'll not rise from your bed before noon at the earliest."

"I know, Aunt Bea, and I am concerned about Jonathan. Even now, I have no time to spend with him."

"'Course not. Told you to hire a tutor."

"I have tried. But the three I've interviewed have been impossible. Jonathan would have hated them."

"Maybe so, but once the young men start buzzing around, you won't have time for the boy."

"I know. With three to chaperon, it will be difficult for the two of us to manage."

"Three? There are four young ladies to chaperon, I'm thinking," Lady Jeffrey said with a smile.

"Really, Aunt Bea, I have been on the shelf too long. Besides, the young gentlemen I've met so far are much too young."

"Puppies, all of them, only suitable for Kitty. But once the Season really gets underway, you'll see."

Abby smiled, but Lady Jeffrey could see resistance in her eyes. "Besides," she added, "I still have my secret. It will ensure our success."

"But you have not revealed your secret," Abby teased. "Are you sure there really is one?"

"Oh, yes, there is one. You'll see it today. We mustn't let a good catch like Lord Harrington get away. He'll make Phoebe a fine husband."

"Don't you think perhaps Lord Harrington might be . . . a little too clever for Phoebe?"

"No, no, of course not. The husband needs to be clever to keep 'em out of the basket. It's the clever kind who always want the most beautiful wife to show off."

"But Aunt Bea, I want the girls to have happy marriages."

"So they will, so they will. But I must have a talk with Monsieur Pierre before Lord Harrington gets here."

"What?" Abby asked, startled. "No, Aunt Bea, I . . . why do you need to talk to Monsieur Pierre?"

"Because I want my lemon cake served when Lord Harrington comes a'calling."

"Your lemon cake? But Aunt Bea, Monsieur Pierre has baked some wonderful French pastries that he will—"

"No. He must serve my lemon cake. And if he refuses, he shall be fired," the old lady said.

Abby didn't want to lose their chef. He was an excellent cook and it would just be one more difficulty to consume her time. "Why don't you let me give instructions to Monsieur Pierre. I can explain to him in French. He is more . . . more agreeable then."

"Well, all right, as long as you make sure he serves it. He was positively impertinent when I was making it. You'd think it was his kitchen," Lady Jeffrey huffed.

Perhaps because, for all practical purposes, it is, Abby thought wryly. Impulsively, she bent to put a kiss on the old lady's rounded cheek. "I shall take care of it, Aunt Bea, and . . . and thank you for caring for us."

"La, child, it's my duty, that's all," Lady Jeffrey protested, her cheeks bright pink.

Abby slipped from the room and Lady Jeffrey watched her go, a smile on her face. What a good child her brother's eldest was. She was glad she would be able to ensure her marriage. It would be a waste for Abigail never to marry and have children of her own.

She sighed as a surge of longing flooded her. She and her Jack had hoped for their own small babe, but it was not to be. Three times she had lost her baby after only a few months. Mayhap God had known she would need to care for her brother's brood. And she would, too. She would see all the girls fired off, and then she and Jonathan would go back to his estate. All it would take was a few morsels of her lemon cake—and all would be right and tight in no time!

MARY SURVEYED her new and growing wardrobe with a critical eye, wanting to look her best this morning. She had had the maid she shared with Kitty put her hair up in rags the night before, and now she was searching for her most ravishing gown.

"Did you ring, Miss Mary?" Rose, her maid, rushed in, her cheeks pink from her rapid climb up the narrow back stairs.

"Oh, Rose, were you busy? I'm sorry but . . . but I need you to do my hair and . . . and what dress shall I wear?"

Rose looked sharply at her favourite mistress. Kitty could be petulant or careless, but Mary was kind and patient. Today, Rose noticed a tension which was generally absent in Mary's voice.

"Certainly, Miss Mary. Perhaps that new lavender morning gown which came yesterday from Madame Emilie?"

"Oh, yes, that would be perfect . . . I think."

"You sit here. I'll take down your hair and fix it all pretty-like and then we'll try the gown."

Under Rose's soothing hands, Mary grew calm, silently berating herself for her silliness. What if Lord Harrington were coming to call this morning? He would take no notice of her. But . . . but if he *should* look her way, she wanted to appear to advantage. Her heart fluttered at such a thought.

Rose, watching her mistress in the looking-glass, saw her lips tremble and wondered what was amiss. She'd ask Mrs. Healy as soon as she returned below stairs.

CHAPTER FOUR

MR. GILES RUSSELL arose from his bed with an unexplained foreboding slowing his movements until he remembered his promise to accompany his cousin on a social visit to the Milhouses. He shrugged off his distaste, refusing to allow such a small thing as that to darken his day. But he had spurned Society for several years. Even such a small step as this would have repercussions.

Ah, well, he had been a little lonely. At least he would have his cousin's company for compensation. And, as if to reinforce that thought, Lord Harrington was already at the breakfast table when Giles entered the dining-room.

"Good morning, Giles. Did you sleep well?"

"Yes, of course, Richard, but I should be asking you that, since I am your host. I did not expect to see you up and about this early."

"I always sleep lightly the first few days in a new place. Soon I will be frittering the day away like most of the ton."

Giles smiled but made no comment as he helped himself to breakfast from the dishes on the sideboard. After sitting down, however, he asked, "You are planning to join in the Season's amusements since you have returned?"

"Yes, of course. There is not much else to do. I am not involved in business, as you are, Giles."

"You have several estates you could see to, Richard. Unless, that is, you have decided to join the married estate."

"I have thought about what you said last night, and you may have a point, Cousin. I think I may be ready to settle down. My latest travels were not as enjoyable as they have been in the past. I believe I am growing old."

"Or perhaps jaded?" Giles asked with a grin.

"Maybe. But if I could find a wife who would delight in those things I enjoy, would not the joy be greater when shared?"

"I am the wrong person to ask such a question, Richard. I was married only a little more than eighteen months and that so many years ago. Alicia and I scarcely had time to get to know each other."

"True. Perhaps you should contemplate matrimony, also."

"No. As I told you last night, I have no desire for a wife. But I wish you joy in yours."

"I want more from you than joy. I trust your judgement more than any man I know, Giles. I want you to help me find a wife."

"What? Why, Richard, that would require . . . I mean, I don't move about much in Society."

"But you know you could, Giles."

Giles grimaced in acknowledgement. "I know, Richard. And I am honoured that you would ask me . . . well, perhaps, after you have discovered a woman you think might be a candidate, I could at least meet her."

"Thank you, Giles. I knew you would not fail me."

"How could I? Thomas is anxious for some cousins. We are a little thin in family, my dear fellow."

"Could I be assured my children would turn out as well as Thomas, I would look forward to expanding the family. He is a fine lad, Giles."

"Yes . . . a little lonesome, I am afraid."

"He has no friends here in London?"

"It is my fault. I cut off all social contact at his birth, and now I scarcely know anyone with children."

"Perhaps a school?"

"Selfishness on my part. I do not want to send him away."

"Hmm. Well, I will try to help keep him company. After all, I mustn't spend all my time flirting with the ladies."

"But you are so good at it," Giles teased and then ducked the biscuit hurled at him by his laughing cousin.

WHEN MARY DESCENDED the stairs in a lavender dress, which flattered her blue eyes and highlighted the gold in her brown hair, her sisters and Aunt Bea were already gathered in the parlour.

"Why, Mary," Abby exclaimed upon her arrival, "how fine you appear. That dress was an excellent choice, dear."

"Thank you, Abby."

"Come sit down, child," Aunt Beatrice ordered. "We were just discussing our day. We will be at home this morning to receive any callers, perhaps Lord Harrington. Later, Abby says she must return to that place to discover a tutor for Jonathan. I thought I would pay a few calls, taking Kitty with me."

"I don't want to go," that young lady said petulantly.

"Kitty," Abby warned, "you will do as your aunt has requested, or you will be sent back to the country while Peter remains here in London."

Other than a dark look, there was no response.

"We wondered if you and Phoebe would care to take Jonathan to see the Elgin Marbles. It will not be as exciting as the Royal Zoo, but at least the boy will get a carriage ride in the bargain."

"You will, of course, take one of the maids and a footman along with you, Mary. Would that be agreeable to you?"

"Yes, of course, Abby, Aunt Bea, if that is what you want."

"Thank you, Mary," Abby said warmly, appreciative of her sister's co-operation.

"What are the Elgin Marbles?" Phoebe asked disinterestedly.

"Who cares?" Kitty said as she flounced down on a sofa.

"They are some ancient ruins brought to England by Lord Elgin," Mary explained.

"Are you sure Jonathan will like that?" Phoebe asked.

"No, but if we are allowed to stop at Gunther's for an ice afterwards, I think he will bear it," Mary assured her sister with a smile.

Abby gave her consent to such an arrangement, adding, "You might even take a turn through the park."

"Yes, Lord Garrett showed a great deal of interest in you, Phoebe, yesterday. It would be well if you saw him in the park again today. He's worth ten thousand a year." Aunt Bea didn't look up from her needle-point to see Phoebe's reaction, but Abby noticed a frown on her sister's face.

"Did you not care for him, dear?"

Phoebe shrugged her shoulders and turned away.

"She's probably hoping to snare Lord Harrington," Kitty said.

The door opened and Healy announced, "Lord Harrington and Mr. Russell."

The family sat frozen, wondering if Kitty's remark had been overheard by their visitors. At the appearance of the two men, Abby rose to greet them. She found herself face to face with Lord Harrington and an unknown gentleman almost as tall as the first. But instead of the handsome countenance Lord Harrington bore, this man had dark bushy eyebrows, black hair and a sombre mien. He watched her approach without a smile.

"How do you do, Miss Milhouse. May I present my cousin, Mr. Giles Russell. He has given me a home for the Season, as I foretold, thereby solving all our problems."

"How do you do, Mr. Russell. Please let me extend our appreciation both to you and Lord Harrington for accommodating us. It would have been sad indeed to find ourselves out in the street." Though she smiled warmly at the tall man, he only acknowledged her words with a half bow and a brief shake of her extended hand.

Abby introduced Mr. Russell to the rest of her family while Lord Harrington greeted everyone in a friendly manner. Abby found it strange that such a congenial man as Lord Harrington should have the withdrawn Mr. Russell for a relative.

When all were seated again, Lord Harrington had quietly manoeuvred his cousin to the seat beside Phoebe, while he availed himself of the seat next to Mary. Not because he was attracted to the young lady, though she was attractive, he admitted, if not in his style. However, she was closest to his cousin and Miss Phoebe. He knew Giles would need assistance in keeping the conversation flowing.

Indeed, neither Phoebe nor Mr. Russell seemed inclined to chat and Mary, seeing signs of distress in Phoebe's face, leaned forward to say, "Your cousin appears to travel a great deal. Do you travel also, Mr. Russell?"

"No, ma'am, I do not. I am involved in business here in the City, and my presence is required."

Mary hid her surprise at such an answer. "Oh, then do you remain in Town the year-round?"

"Almost. I take my son to one of our estates for periodic visits."

Abby leaned forward eagerly. "You have a son, Mr. Russell? How old is he?"

Frowning as if he resented such a personal question, Mr. Russell answered her, "He is nine, Miss Milhouse."

"Our brother Jonathan is eight. Is your son as active as Jonathan?" Abby asked with a reminiscent smile on her face.

Recognizing her train of thought, Giles relaxed. "Yes, he is quite active, wouldn't you say so, Richard?"

"Indeed. The vase he broke last night rushing to greet me was priceless. I shall have to return to the Orient to replace it."

"You have been to the Orient?" Mary gasped in wonder.

"Yes. It was quite an experience."

"Is it far away?" Phoebe asked blankly.

Lord Harrington was stunned by the question, and Mary hurried to assist her sister. "You were not paying attention, dear. Lord Harrington said the Orient, which, of course, is terribly far away."

"Oh. Yes, of course."

As Lord Harrington and his cousin exchanged looks, Healy appeared at the door with a second pair of callers. One of these was greeted much more enthusiastically than the previous ones.

"Peter!" Kitty exclaimed, rising to rush to the slender young man who followed Healy. "It has taken you forever to arrive in London. Did you just get here?"

Healy cleared his throat and said, "Lord Abbott and Sir William Bost."

Abby, with a warning glance to her sister, rose to greet the two new arrivals. "Peter, how lovely to see you again. May I present my aunt, Lady Jeffrey? And Sir William, I am Miss Milhouse, a neighbour of Peter's, so I hope you will forgive our informality."

"'Course I will. Peter told me all about you. Matter of fact, just call me Willie. I ain't much for formality myself."

"Why, uh, thank you, Willie. May I make you acquainted with Lord Harrington and Mr. Russell? Gentlemen, Sir William Bost and this is Lord Abbott, a near neighbour of ours."

Kitty grabbed Peter's arm and dragged him to a seat next to her. "Did you just arrive?" she asked again.

"No, I got here last week, but Willie—"

"What?" Kitty screamed in shock.

"Kitty, you forget yourself." Abby's warning reached its target and Kitty drew a deep breath before she continued.

"I have been waiting each day for your arrival. Why did you not let me know you were here?"

"Willie told me I had to get rigged out. Couldn't go around looking like a country bumpkin."

Kitty shot a look of intense dislike toward her intended's friend, but he took no notice of it. He had discovered Phoebe's golden beauty and was staring at her in reverential silence.

Abby rose to ring for tea, hoping refreshments would save the occasion, which was rapidly deteriorating into a disaster. Healy had everything in readiness and only several more minutes of disjointed conversation occurred before the door was opened and he entered with the tea tray, followed by several footmen bearing additional delicacies.

Lady Jeffrey eyed the trays. There, on the second tray, were slices of her lemon cake on delicate china. But they were surrounded by the pastries concocted by that French chef. Instead of waiting to be served by her nieces, Lady Jeffrey pushed her rounded form up from the chair where she had been sewing, dropping thread, needle, pin cushion and the handkerchief she had been hemming, all over the floor. Sublimely ignoring the shower of articles, she sailed over to Abby while everyone else stared.

"I shall deliver the tea, my dear," she assured her eldest niece.

"Why, of course, Aunt Bea, if you wish to, but Mary or Kitty could—"

"No, I am determined to do so." So saying, she whisked away the first cup filled and then paused to take a dish of lemon cake over to Lord Harrington.

"Uh, thank you, dear ma'am, but ladies first, of course."

She stared at him blankly before saying, "Drat! Of course." She thrust the cup and saucer into Phoebe's lap and returned the plate of lemon cake to the tray. Abby stared at her, her pouring halted in surprise, until her aunt reminded her of her duties.

Abby poured the cups of tea and Aunt Bea gave the other two girls a cup before she took the next cup and the same piece of lemon cake and returned to Lord Harrington. "Here you go, my lord. A special treat for you."

Lord Harrington took her offering with a smile, wondering if insanity ran in their family. He watched the lady offer the same to his cousin.

"This cake is a family tradition, you know," she said chattily, sitting down and ignoring their two other guests. "I prepared it myself."

"I'd like to try some," Sir William put in, his rounded form giving evidence to his partiality to sweets.

"Of course, Sir William," Abby said, having already passed cups to him and Peter. But Lady Jeffrey rushed to the tray to take a French pastry and give it to the young man. "Nay, you would not like it, I'm sure, Mr.....uh, I mean, Sir William. You must try the pastries our French chef prepared. I'm sure you will enjoy them."

Mary and Abby exchanged a speaking look but presented serene smiles to the guests. Each initiated conversation with their neighbour, Abby to Sir William and Mary to Lord Harrington, and Abby smiled at Phoebe encouragingly.

Giles Russell, having watched the serving of the tea with barely restrained laughter, caught Abby's smile to her sister and thought it a lovely one. He also recognized it as encouragement to his companion to engage him in conversation. When she said nothing, his pity for her caused him to come to her aid.

"Does your young brother attend a school here in London or does he have a tutor?"

"N-neither, my lord. Abby is trying to find a tutor, but she says they are all fubsy-faced and Jonathan would not like them."

"Ah. It can be a difficult chore to find a good tutor. I am fortunate that my son has a tutor he both admires and enjoys and yet learns something also."

Abby could not help but overhear their conversation as she was seated nearby. With a pardon to Sir William, she leaned toward Mr. Russell. "Could you tell me where to find just such a paragon as yours, Mr. Russell? I am quite desperate."

"I'm afraid I cannot, Miss Milhouse. I discovered Charles Brownlee quite by accident. But I agree that he is a paragon." An idea was taking shape in Mr. Russell's mind, but he wanted some assurances before he committed himself. "How does your brother entertain himself while you are otherwise occupied?"

"By getting in the servants' way and causing turmoil," Abby replied with a warm chuckle.

"Perhaps he might care to pay a visit to Thomas this afternoon? I believe Charles has planned a visit to the park to see a balloon ascension."

"Why, that would be wonderful, Mr. Russell, if you are sure your Mr. Brownlee would not object to the added responsibility. Jonathan is well-behaved, but...but well, you know how little boys are."

"Quite, Miss Milhouse. I promise Mr. Brownlee will keep an eye on him."

"Phoebe and Mary were going to take him to see the Elgin Marbles. I'm sure he will prefer a balloon ascension."

"Balloon ascension?" Sir William said, catching the last of their conversation. "I say, that's a capital idea. Where did you say it was to be held?"

"I'm not sure, Sir William. I would have to enquire of my son's tutor for the exact location."

"By George, Peter! Did you hear that? There's to be a balloon ascension today. Shall we go?"

Peter, having been chastised for his neglect of his beloved, glanced hesitantly at her before answering his old school friend. "Well..."

"I should enjoy seeing a balloon ascension, Peter," Kitty said imperiously.

"Not a place for young ladies," Sir William assured her.

Abby was amused until Sir William said that. "Are you sure it will be suitable for the children?" she asked Mr. Russell.

"Of course, ma'am. Many of Society will be there, especially as the weather is so fine today."

"Oh, I would love to see it," Mary said. "I read about the mechanics of it, but to actually see it rise into the air..."

Lord Harrington gallantly responded to Mary's implied invitation. "I would be pleased to escort you, Miss Mary, and Miss Phoebe, also. I might even persuade my cousin to accompany us."

Mary flushed with pleasure. Before she could ask Abby for permission to accept, Mr. Russell decided it would be best to make it a family party rather than allow himself to be paired off with the lovely Miss Phoebe. "Why don't we all go?"

Everyone but Lady Jeffrey seemed eager to be a member of the party, though Sir William still said he didn't think ladies should be there. He feared they might faint from the excitement.

"Never," Kitty assured him scornfully.

"I'll ask our chef to put up a basket of refreshments to bring along," Abby inserted, hoping to avert an argument. "Little boys need frequent feeding."

Giles Russell decided Abby's smile was her best feature. If her brother was as agreeable as his sister, he thought his plan might work.

"You have not eaten your cake, Mr. Russell," Lady Jeffrey suddenly gasped.

"Why, no, ma'am. I'm afraid I don't have much of a sweet tooth."

"I'll eat it. No point in letting it go to waste," Sir William said, reaching for the untouched plate.

"That you won't!" Lady Jeffrey cried as she rushed to snatch the plate from his fingertips. "You've had your share," she added with a sniff.

Abby, horrified by her aunt's behaviour, apologized quickly. "I am sorry, Sir William. It . . . it is an acquired taste. I'll have our chef prepare some particular delicacies for you for the balloon ascension."

"Thank you, Miss Milhouse," Sir William said with an air of wounded dignity. "What time shall we return?"

Abby turned questioning eyes to Mr. Russell, who said, "I believe the ascension is to be at four o'clock. Shall we assemble here at three?"

Everyone agreed and the gentlemen departed, breaking into their original pairs once they reached the street. Lord Abbott and Sir William hurried away on foot, determined to discover the proper attire for watching a balloon ascension, and Lord Harrington and Mr. Russell ascended to the latter's curricle. The tiger scrambled to jump up behind after turning loose the matched greys.

"A most interesting visit," Giles said as he guided his horses through the busy streets.

"Lord, yes. The aunt was deuced odd, didn't you think?"

"Some women seem to grow more so as they approach old age."

"True, but she certainly behaved oddly about the cake. Did you taste it? Terrible!"

"No, I did not. I do not generally care for sweets, and I must admit that cake did nothing to tempt me."

"Ah, well, the young ladies are lovely. Though the beauty did not appear too bright."

"One cannot be blessed with all things," Mr. Russell murmured to his cousin.

"AUNT BEA, are you feeling quite the thing?" Abby asked as soon as their guests had departed.

"Why, yes, of course, my dear. And things turned out well, did they not?"

"I suppose so. You do not mind accompanying us to the ascension?"

"Well, I do not care to dine alfresco, but I suppose I can do so for your sakes. After all, we must develop our friendship with two such eligible men."

"Do you mean Lord Harrington and Mr. Russell, or Sir William and Lord Abbott?" Abby asked with a smile.

"Faugh! That Sir William is useless. Much too young, except for Kitty, and she's already got Lord Abbott. Though I can see why you put off their engagement. Not got much backbone, does he?"

Kitty, who had been discussing their plans with her sisters, heard her aunt's last remark. "Who? Surely you are not talking about Peter?"

"Never mind." replied Abby. "You and I are going to discuss your behaviour this morning. If you will excuse us, Aunt Bea? And Mary, if you could inform Jonathan of the treat in store for him, I would appreciate it. Come, Kitty."

With Abby's words, the family dispersed to prepare for the afternoon's outing.

CHAPTER FIVE

ABBY HOPED her talk with Kitty would ensure more lady-like behaviour that afternoon as they all met for the balloon ascension. But secretly, she couldn't help sympathizing with her youngest sister. It was a shock to Kitty to discover that her faithful follower might shift his allegiance. Should Peter continue to do as Willie advised rather than ask his beloved's opinion, Abby was sure more private talks with Kitty would be necessary.

Lady Jeffrey entered the parlour where the four young ladies and Jonathan awaited the others. "Well, you are all well turned-out. I suppose if we must go, we should do it in style."

"Aunt, truly, if you don't want to go, I can chaperon our little party," Abby offered.

"And who would chaperon you?" her aunt asked. "There are four gentlemen coming and four of you."

"Sir William doesn't count," Kitty said stiffly. "He's only a hanger-on."

"Kitty," Abby warned.

"You are wrong, my dear," Lady Jeffrey said. "I discovered his family is quite well-to-do. He is a most eligible *parti*. I was wrong not to serve him some of my lemon cake. He will do nicely for Mary."

Poor Mary blanched at a pairing so far from her dreams. Even Phoebe could not imagine the two as a couple.

"I think Mary would be better suited to Lord Harrington. They are both so clever."

Abby was struck by Phoebe's wisdom and her realization was reinforced when she saw Mary duck her head. Her disappointment with herself that she had not recognized such an obvious thing was curtailed by the arrival of Lord Abbott and Sir William.

Kitty greeted both gentlemen coldly and it was left to the others to entertain them. But Abby was still thinking about Phoebe's remark. If Lord Harrington was for Mary, who would Phoebe . . . of course, Mr. Russell. He seemed nice enough. And as tender-hearted as Phoebe was, she would make a loving mother.

The arrival of that gentleman and his cousin, accompanied by his young son, interrupted her thoughts. She measured him with her eyes next to the fragile beauty of her sister. She almost decided his features were too harsh until he smiled as he bowed over Phoebe's hand.

Abby's thoughts were interrupted by a small hand stealing into hers and her brother's voice whispering, "Abby, what's his name?"

"What? Oh, Jonathan, I don't know." She turned back to Mr. Russell, whose son was staying close to his side. "Mr. Russell, may I present my brother, Jonathan."

Giles Russell turned to the young lady and brought forth his shy son. "My pleasure, Master Jonathan. Permit me to present my son, Thomas."

The two boys eyed each other warily. Abby, with a smile she quickly hid, suggested both boys join her on the settee and began a conversation by asking gentle questions to draw Thomas out. When both boys found the common ground of enthusiasm for the balloon ascension, she was able to retire from their conversation. She was surprised to discover Mr. Russell watching her with an approving smile.

Her cheeks hot, Abby stood to organize their departure.

"Is it time already?" Lady Jeffrey complained.

"Yes, Aunt, if we are to arrive before the ascension. Mary, would you ring the bell and ask Healy to put the baskets of food in the carriage? With the baskets, we can only take four in our carriage. Do any of you gentlemen have room for more passengers, or shall we order a second carriage?"

"We came in Willie's high-perch phaeton," Peter said nervously, watching Kitty out of the corner of his eye.

Rather than exploding, Kitty stared at him icily before turning a warm smile on Lord Harrington. "Do you have room for me, my lord? I promise I do not take up much room." With her eyelashes fanning her cheeks rapidly, Kitty waited for his response.

"Of course, Miss Kitty. We brought the laudalet and it holds six passengers."

Aware of Mary's interest, Abby suggested, "If you do not mind, Mr. Russell, Thomas may ride with Jonathan, Lady Jeffrey and myself, if you and Lord Harrington would escort my three sisters."

"We will be delighted to accompany such charming young ladies. I'm sure we will be the envy of all the young bucks," Lord Harrington assured her.

As they took their places in the vehicles, Lord Abbott looked longingly at Kitty, who purposely flirted with Lord Harrington. Mary gave no sign of distress other than her silence. Abby groaned. She could already foresee another lecture to Kitty.

The two boys were cautiously advancing their friendship, and Abby was impressed with Thomas's deportment, thinking that if any of his quiet manners were to rub off on Jonathan, it would be a good thing.

"I thought Lord Abbott and Kitty were a couple. Why is she making eyes at Lord Harrington?" Lady Jeffrey asked.

With a warning look at young Thomas, Abby said, "It's only a small tiff, Aunt. There was no room in Sir William's phaeton for an additional person."

"Those things are dangerous. No woman of reason would ride in one."

"Papa says they are very safe, my lady," Thomas said hesitantly.

Though Lady Jeffrey glared at the boy, Abby smiled. "I'm sure you are right, Thomas. At least, you are if the driver knows how to handle his horses. Does your father have a high-perch phaeton?"

"Yes, Miss Milhouse. Sometimes he takes me for rides."

"I wish I had a father," Jonathan muttered, envy in his eyes. "I only get to do girl things."

Abby wanted to protest her brother's indictment of her care, but since their arrival in the city, he was almost right. "I don't consider the Royal Zoo a girl thing, Jonathan," she said gently.

"I have not been there in several years. Is the lion still there?" Thomas asked enthusiastically. Abby and Lady Jeffrey exchanged smiles as the two boys eagerly made comparisons of their visits.

Their arrival at Regent's Park was noted by groups of friends and acquaintances and several young bucks whose eyes were caught by the three young ladies in Mr. Russell's carriage. It seemed all of London had decided to attend the ascension.

Before the two gentlemen could assist the ladies in their descent, they found themselves surrounded by friends and acquaintances.

"Richard! We did not expect to see you this Season. Were you not off to foreign parts?" Lord Hanscom demanded as he slapped his friend on the shoulder. But his eyes were trained on Lord Harrington's guests.

Several others echoed his sentiments, but one paused to stare at the quiet man standing beside Lord Harrington. "As I live and breathe, it's Giles Russell! It's good to see you, man. How are you?"

Momentarily, the young women were forgotten as several of the men greeted Mr. Russell. One man, however, was not surprised by his existence, only by his appearance among the ton.

"Giles, I am pleased to see you socializing again. Have you had a change of heart?"

Mr. Russell grimaced and lowered his voice. "Only because my cousin has joined me for the Season, Jason. He's a social creature by nature."

"Doesn't Lord Harrington have his own town house, a rather elegant affair on Mulberry Square?"

"Yes, but it is currently occupied by the charming ladies accompanying us, the Misses Milhouse, through his agent's duplicity."

"Ah, yes, the ladies. They are what drew me to you in the first place."

"Why, Jason, I did not know you were in the petticoat line."

"No more than you, dear Giles," he said with a grin. "Will you present me?"

"With pleasure."

The two gentlemen, one tall and dark, the other of medium height with light brown hair frosted on his sideburns, rejoined the others grouped around the carriage.

"May we help you descend from the carriage, ladies, to join your sister and aunt?" Mr. Russell asked.

Kitty jumped up to be first, followed by Mary and Phoebe. As each was helped down, Mr. Russell presented his friend, Lord Norfolk. Kitty flirted outrageously with him while her eyes searched for Peter. Mary greeted him and then he turned to Phoebe. Though he was easily twenty years older than that young lady, Lord Norfolk appeared struck by her golden beauty.

Lord Harrington turned back to the group and introduced more gentlemen desirous of meeting the young ladies. Abby and Aunt Bea watched from their carriage. "I should not say so, but it was great good fortune that we leased Lord Harrington's house and he returned unexpectedly," Abby confessed.

"That is true, my love. You should be over there being introduced also, however, not stuck here with an old woman and children."

"I have no complaints, Aunt Bea." Abby turned back to watch the scene unfolding before her. With a frown, she noted an older man talking to Phoebe. "Who is that gentleman, Aunt Bea? The one talking to Phoebe."

The old lady leaned forward, her eyes straining. "I don't know, child. We must find out. It is up to us to keep the girls' reputations safe."

"Surely, Lord Harrington and Mr. Russell would not—" Abby halted abruptly as she realized the boys' conversation had ended and Thomas was watching her. She smiled at the child and said, "I'm sure everything is as it should be. Perhaps we might—"

"Miss Milhouse, are you and your aunt ready to join the others?" Mr. Russell asked, causing Abby to start guiltily.

"Oh . . . yes, sir, that would be . . . yes, we are ready."

Mr. Russell assisted the two women to the grassy carpet and smiled as the boys scrambled down from the carriage.

"I trust this young scamp behaved himself?" he asked, gesturing toward his son.

"He was a perfect gentleman, Mr. Russell. We enjoyed his company very much," Abby assured him, smiling warmly at Thomas.

"Papa, may Jonathan and I go closer to the balloon?"

"If it is all right with his sister."

Abby turned from the eager looks of the two boys to Mr. Russell. "Are you sure it will be quite safe?"

"Of course. Thomas knows to stay out of the way. He has been to other ascensions."

"Well, all right, but, Jonathan, stay with Thomas and don't be away too long."

Scarcely were the words out of her mouth before the two boys were off at a run. Abby stared after them.

"They will be fine, Miss Milhouse, I promise."

Abby turned to smile apologetically. "I know, Mr. Russell, but I cannot seem to keep from being anxious."

He offered her his arm with no response but a smile and turned to offer the other to Lady Jeffrey. He gave quiet orders to the servants about spreading out the robes and pillows brought for the picnic and led the ladies over to the others.

Abby soon discovered the identity of the older man. Mr. Russell presented Lord Norfolk to her as an old friend, and though she found nothing offensive about him, it was clear he was a man of experience and considerably older than she would wish one of Phoebe's suitors to be.

However, her mind was more immediately taken up with Kitty, who had surrounded herself with seven or eight handsome young men. She was distributing her attention evenly, smiling and flashing her eyes at every one of them. Abby realized something must be done or she would be considered fast. "Kitty, could you assist me with the picnic?" she called.

Kitty strolled over, accompanied by her entourage, but showed no interest in assisting. "Kitty, I believe you should sit down before you wear yourself out," Abby said pointedly. The young lady glared at her older sister before turning to bid her new friends *adieu*. Then she flounced down upon the cushions.

Mr. Russell knelt beside Abby and whispered, "Would you object to my asking Lord Norfolk to join us? He is a close friend."

Abby wanted to protest, but she felt obliged to give in to Mr. Russell's request. In no time at all, Lord Norfolk had taken a place next to Phoebe, while Sir William was on her other side.

The other members of their party joined them on the robes, Lord Abbott claiming the seat beside Kitty. Mary moved to help her sister pass around the food and drinks, and Phoebe stared about her at the numerous parties.

"There must be hundreds of people here. Who would have thought that many would be interested in such a thing?

"Ballooning is an amazing feat, Miss Phoebe. Imagine soaring over the trees like a bird. Would you not want to do that?"

She stared at Mr. Russell blankly. "Good heavens, no. Why would I?"

Lord Norfolk smiled blandly at his friend. "Of course not, Giles. That is too dangerous for ladies."

"It would not be too dangerous for me," Kitty assured them.

"I have heard of terrible accidents occurring to balloonists," Lord Harrington said, "but I must admit I would like to give it a try."

"Have you never done so? I thought with your many travels you might have gone ballooning," Mary said wistfully.

"No, I never have. Most of the places I've been have no advanced society as we have here in England or on the Continent, other than in small areas. Certainly on the seaboard in America there are some sophisticated cities, but beyond them, it is wilderness. That is where I spent most of my time."

Several others asked questions that kept Lord Harrington talking of his travels. While Kitty and Phoebe showed no interest, Lord Harrington noticed Mary's eager questions and the deep interest in her blue eyes.

The boys' return brought the conversation back to the ascension as they eagerly explained everything they had seen. Only when Abby offered them food did they stop their dialogue. She watched the two of them move off by themselves to indulge in the treats provided, talking back and forth about the things they had seen. It would be good for Jonathan to have a friend here in London.

Mr. Russell also watched the boys for several minutes before making a decision. He moved around the rug to seat himself next to Miss Milhouse.

"I think I have a proposition to put to you, Miss Milhouse," he said, without thinking about the possible connotation of his words, until he looked up to see Abby staring at him in horror, her cheeks flaming.

"No! No, I did not mean—" he broke off, turning as red as the young woman next to him.

"I say, Mr. Russell, what are you saying to my niece?" Lady Jeffrey demanded from the other side of the circle.

"It was a misunderstanding. I did not mean to...that is, I was discussing my son's education."

There were several chuckles at such an inane answer, but no further questions were asked. Mr. Russell remained silent until the others drifted off into other conversation. Then he said quietly, "I apologize for my social ineptness, Miss Milhouse. I have been used to having business discussions only for a long period of time."

"It is of no matter," Abby muttered, unable to look at her neighbour.

"I truly was discussing my son's education. That is, I was about to offer, well, to suggest that you allow Jonathan to come to my home each day and share Thomas's classes. You have said you were having difficulty finding a good tutor, and I can assure you Mr. Brownlee is an excellent one."

"Oh, no. That is generous of you, Mr. Russell, but we could not allow you . . ."

"But you would be helping me also, Miss Milhouse. You see, I have cut myself off from the social world, and Thomas has no friends his own age with whom to play. He and Jonathan seem to enjoy each other's company, so it would provide Thomas with a companion."

Abby looked up into Mr. Russell's green eyes, the only similarity between him and his cousin, and saw there the sincerity of his offer. "If . . . if you are sure it will not discommode you, or Mr. Brownlee, it would be a wonderful answer to my problem. But only if you allow me to pay a part of Mr. Brownlee's wages."

"It would be of great assistance to me. And if you propose to pay Mr. Brownlee anything for his efforts on Jonathan's behalf, that is no concern of mine."

"May I meet Mr. Brownlee? Could he call on me when it is convenient to discuss such a plan?"

"Of course, Miss Milhouse. I will send him round first thing tomorrow. Will that be satisfactory?"

"Yes, that would be—"

"Look!" Jonathan shrieked. "It's rising!"

Everyone turned in the direction Jonathan was point-ing to see the balloon growing in size. "They are filling the balloon with hot air," Thomas said importantly. "May we go back to watch, Papa?"

With Abby's reluctant permission, Mr. Russell sent the two boys on their way. The others sat quietly watching the spectacle until they were disturbed by an unladylike snore emanating from Lady Jeffrey.

"Poor Aunt Bea," Mary said with a smile. "She really has no interest in ballooning."

"Neither do I," Phoebe said. "I shall enjoy the balls much more."

"Do you like dancing, Miss Phoebe?" Lord Norfolk asked.

"Oh, yes. It is a glorious thing, do you not think so?"

"With you as my partner, I'm sure it will be. May I request the honour of a dance with you at your first ball?"

"And me, too!" Sir William demanded, trying to maintain ground against this latecomer for Miss Phoebe's interest.

"But you are both silly. I do not know when our first ball will be."

Lord Norfolk said, "The first ball of the Season is Lady Mayberry's. Did you receive cards?"

"I don't know. Abby, did we receive invitations to Lady Mayberry's ball?"

"Why, yes, we did, Phoebe. Why?"

"Oh, these gentlemen have requested dances at the first ball I attend. Lord Norfolk says it will be Lady Mayber-ry's."

Abby's eyes slid from Phoebe's innocent face to that of Lord Norfolk before saying coolly, "Yes, that will be the first ball we attend."

"Then you may both have a dance," Phoebe said happily.

Lord Norfolk lifted Phoebe's hand and carried it briefly to his lips. "Thank you, sweet lady. I shall await the moment with great anticipation."

He ignored the dark look Abby cast towards him.

"BUT ABBY, he is so very kind."

"I'm sure he is, Phoebe, dear, but he is also ever so much older than you. Why, he is almost as old as Papa would be, had he lived. I do not mind that you have given him a dance. Just . . . just be careful."

"Of course I will be careful, Abby. It is only a dance. I also gave one to Sir William."

"Yes, you did, love, and he was most pleased."

"Yes, but I don't think I will enjoy it. He does not appear to be very graceful."

"There will be others there who will be able to sweep you across the floor. I'm sure you will be the belle of the ball."

With a smile, Phoebe ran up the stairs, and Abby turned back into the parlour with a frown on her face.

"What is it, Abby?" Mary asked.

"Oh, Mary, I do not know. Things grow so complicated."

"Is it Mr. Russell? He did not offend you at the picnic, did he?"

Abby smiled in mockery of her blushes. "No, love. I should have known better, but he . . . never mind. He truly was speaking to me about Thomas's education. He offered to let Jonathan share Thomas's tutor. It is a wonderful thing, because now I do not have to interview any more horrid men totally unsuited to the teaching of small boys. And I think Jonathan will enjoy it very much.''

"How wonderful. I will be glad to walk Jonathan to Mr. Russell's house each day, if you wish.''

"That is kind of you, dear, but—''

"It is very near here.''

"How do you know that?''

With her cheeks flushed, Mary studied the pattern her finger was unconsciously tracing on her skirt. "I asked Lord Harrington.''

"I see. Well, perhaps, occasionally, you may walk Jonathan to Mr. Russell's house, with a maid accompanying you, of course. But most of the time, I believe it would be best if we had one of the footmen take him.''

"Oh.''

"Darling Mary...don't set your heart on Lord Harrington. He—''

"Oh, no, Abby! I would never—''

"He seems a wonderful man, my sweet, but I'm sure he is pursued by the most eligible young ladies. While your dowry is respectable, I do not think—''

"I was only being friendly, Abby, truly. I know—that is, he is a most attractive man, but I know he is not for me. I suspect he is smitten with Phoebe. He—he watched her a lot today at the picnic. She looked truly beautiful in her blue gown with the matching ribbons in her h-hair,'' Mary managed to say before a sob slipped out.

"Oh, darling,'' Abby said consolingly as she walked over and put her arms around her dearest sister. "I am beginning to wish we had never come to London. And the Season has not even yet begun.''

CHAPTER SIX

"Is MY GOWN not exquisite?" Phoebe demanded with a laugh as she whirled around her bedchamber.

"Yes, dear, it is, as are you," Abby assured her. When Phoebe had resumed her seat in front of the looking-glass to determine if her cavorting had disturbed her spun-gold curls, Abby said, "You seem much happier now than when we first came to London."

"Oh, yes. I grew so tired of all the visits, the endless conversations. They made me feel so stupid."

"Phoebe! Surely you are mistaken. No one would try to make you appear to disadvantage."

"Oh, not on purpose, Abby. But you know how easy it is for Mary, or you, or even Kitty, to discourse at length on any subject. I have no interest in government or travel or things of that sort. I want to talk about balls and gowns and...and love," she said almost defiantly.

"Love?"

"Oh, Abby, do not fuss. I am not really in love, but...it is delicious to be courted and admired and to dance the night away."

"You've had so much experience of such?" Abby ignored her sister's pout. "You must be on your best behaviour this evening, Phoebe. Gracious! This sounds like the conversation I had earlier with Kitty. What is happening to our family!"

The concern in Abby's voice touched Phoebe and she ran to throw her arms around her. "We are just—just expanding, Abby. It will be all right, I promise. I will not disgrace you."

"As if you could, my love. I'm sorry to be such a worry-wart. Now, straighten your skirts and join us downstairs. I am just going to look in on Mary."

Abby closed Phoebe's door and leant against it to regain her composure. Even though she also had a charming new gown for the evening, in an icy blue, she did not have the enthusiasm Phoebe had shown. She was too concerned about her sisters' debut this evening. Much hinged on how well Society welcomed them.

With a sigh, she moved on to Mary's door. She knew she did not have to warn Mary about her behaviour. She mostly wanted to lend a little moral support to her beloved sister. Mary had struggled to hide her tender heart and Abby hoped tonight would not prove too difficult for her.

She had heard that Lord Harrington had received an invitation for the evening, as was to be expected, but whether he had accepted was not known. Since their initial meeting, she had become aware of the young man's popularity and knew her sister would only be one of many of his admirers.

She discovered Mary seated in front of her mirror also, and Abby was pleased with how well her sister looked.

"Mary, dear, you are beautiful!"

Colour flamed in Mary's cheeks as she jumped up to embrace her sister. "Nonsense, Abby. It is only the dress."

With a smile, Abby said, "You are wrong, my love. You are enchanting in your pale green foam, but it is the smile that makes you beautiful."

With a shrug, Mary tried to hide her agitation. "I hope—I hope I am passable, anyway. I am looking forward to this evening. Are not you, Abby? And you look wonderful in your gown, too."

"Thank you, my love. Shall we go down? I'm sure Aunt Bea is already awaiting us."

LADY JEFFREY was not only awaiting them but was also prepared to scold them for their tardiness. "You must not waste your time primping here where no one can see you. Let us be on our way."

No one argued with her reasoning and after a short carriage ride and a long wait in line for their carriage to reach Lady Mayberry's steps, they arrived at their first ball.

Though Phoebe was doubtless the most beautiful of the four sisters, they made an impressive sight arriving together, four well turned-out young ladies. It was unheard-of for a family to try to fire off four daughters at once, so they drew considerable attention.

Lady Jeffrey led the way in much the same way a mother duck guided her babies to the water. A long acquaintance with Lady Mayberry would make the evening a pleasant one for her, catching up on the news of friends, and she was eager to see her protegées in action among the elegant bachelors of the ton. It was important that they make a good impression because she could not serve lemon cake to eligible bachelors unless the girls received visits. Casting a shrewd eye over her charges, she was reassured.

Lady Jeffrey felt even more at ease after the first half-hour. Many young men had found someone to introduce them to the four young ladies and their dance cards had rapidly filled. Abby was relieved to see that Phoebe was granting dances to many different young men and had not yet been approached by Lord Norfolk. In fact, neither he nor the two other more mature gentlemen had appeared at the ball. Abby knew Mary was watching out of the corner of her eye for Lord Harrington's arrival, but he and his cousin seemed to have chosen another entertainment that evening.

Kitty was enthusiastically granting dances to all those men who asked, but Abby could detect a stiffness to her shoulders that showed her anger with Peter. Poor Peter. If he were torn between Kitty and his friend, Sir William, for the entire season, he would be miserable.

"I hope you have saved me a dance, Miss Milhouse," a deep voice said, distracting Abby from her thoughts. She turned to discover Mr. Russell at her elbow.

"Mr. Russell. Good evening, I was just . . . yes, I have a dance available. But you should hurry if you are to have a dance with Phoebe. I'm sure her card will soon be filled."

"All in good time. I thought we might discuss our joint venture in education," the man said with a warm smile, his eyes surveying her elegant appearance.

Abby saw Lord Harrington talking with Phoebe while Mr. Russell signed her card, and she understood the man's lack of concern. Of course, he would not compete with his own cousin. Her eyes sought out Mary, hoping she would not wear her heart on her sleeve, but she discovered her sister talking with a man only an inch or two taller than she, with a thick waistline and receding hair.

"Mr. Russell, do you know the identity of the gentleman conversing with Mary?"

Giles glanced over in Mary's direction before turning back to Abby. "That's Mr. Morrison. He's a remote connection of the Earl of Vye and serves as his secretary."

"Thank you. I find it a disadvantage that I have so few acquaintances in London when I must chaperon my sisters."

Mr. Russell was startled. "You think of yourself as a chaperon?"

"Why, yes, of course," Abby answered without much thought, while she kept her three sisters in view. "Mother made me their legal guardian before her death."

"But Lady Jeffrey said all four of you are making your debuts this season."

"Well, that is true," Abby said almost shamefacedly. "I mean, I have never before attended a Season in London, but I am not...that is, I have no...I do not expect to marry. Oh, dear."

Mr. Russell, finding himself more entertained by Miss Milhouse's conversation than he had ever imagined he could be, was brought up short by her last remark. "Is something amiss, Miss Milhouse?"

Abby, watching Lord Norfolk sign Phoebe's card twice, stopped herself before confiding her dislike of her sister's suitor, even though Mr. Russell seemed uncommonly easy to talk to. "No, of course not, Mr. Russell."

She was saved from further explanation by the arrival of her first partner, a young man years younger than she, who made her feel even more motherly. "Good evening, Mr. Brownhurst. Are you acquainted with Mr. Russell?"

The two gentlemen shook hands and Mr. Brownhurst led his partner eagerly away. Abby had assumed he asked her to dance out of politeness, but she misjudged her partner. The young man had been struck by her angelic fairness and chose her above all three of her sisters. Abby would have been quite surprised had she known.

The four sisters formed a set for the country dance that opened the ball, Abby with Mr. Brownhurst, Mary with Mr. Morrison, Phoebe and Kitty with partners unknown to Abby. But because both appeared quite young and harmless, Abby was able to relax and enjoy the dance.

She had originally intended to remain against the wall as a chaperon, but a discussion with her aunt had forced her to change her mind.

Aunt Beatrice assured her she would be humiliated to have one of her charges considered a wallflower; or worse, that the ton would think Abby did not consider her aunt a sufficient chaperon for four green girls. That left Abby with no option but to accept all invitations, and to her surprise, she had only several unsigned dances on her card.

Mary, a graceful dancer, forced herself to concentrate on her steps and not on the tall gentleman who had signed her dance card just before the music had begun. Lord Harrington had arrived only a few minutes ago and had come across the ballroom at once. However, since he first signed Phoebe's card, Mary found no happiness to be gained from that fact. Now, she knew he and his cousin, Mr. Russell, were standing talking to Aunt Bea, but she strove to give no indication that she had noticed it.

"THEY ARE an impressive quartet, Lady Jeffrey," Lord Harrington said as he watched the Milhouse ladies dance.

"Yes, and they are good girls, too," the elderly lady replied feelingly.

"But is it not difficult to fire off so many in one Season?"

"It might not be my choice in the normal course of things, my lord, but I can assure you it would have been impossible to leave any of them at home."

Both gentlemen exchanged amused smiles, recognizing the truth in the woman's statement. Mr. Russell, wondering at the lady's reaction, said, "Miss Milhouse tells me she is not actually seeking marriage."

"What?" Lady Jeffrey shrieked before hiding her embarrassment behind her old-fashioned fan. "Pay no attention to her, Mr. Russell. She feels responsible for the others and nothing I do or say can persuade her that she is also a child.''

Lord Harrington changed the subject to the latest on-dit, and Lady Jeffrey, who enjoyed a good gossip, followed his lead. Mr. Russell cast his eye on Miss Milhouse, his mind still on their previous conversation. Lady Jeffrey was wrong. She was not a child. And yet, there was a freshness, a warmth, that assured all who met her that she had not been "out" before now. Certainly, she was not beyond marriageable age. He hoped she found an eligible parti. It would be a shame for her not to become a mother.

"SCOOT OVER, KITTY, you are squashing me," Phoebe complained as they returned home from their first ball. In contrast to the excited chatter that had filled their trip to Lady Mayberry's, most were now silent.

"I am not! You are just—"

"Girls, please!" Abby begged. "Aunt Bea is asleep and you must not disturb her. She is—"

"If you say old, my girl, you will be in trouble," Lady Jeffrey said with a chuckle, her eyes still closed.

"Never, Aunt Bea," Abby said warmly, her mind frantically searching for a substitute. "I was only going to say that you were not used to these late nights."

Mary yawned. "Neither am I."

"But it was worth it!" Phoebe enthused. "I had a wonderful time."

"I should think so, child," Lady Jeffrey said. "You danced every dance and had them begging for more."

"I could have danced every dance," Kitty asserted in irritation. "But I saved two dances for Peter." Everyone could hear the dire threat in her voice that said she would render punishment the next time she encountered that young man.

"We were all quite well-received," Abby said, "and it is rude to boast."

"Oh, Abby, it is just among us." Phoebe sighed happily before adding, "This is what I thought London would be, not all that dull visiting."

"We still must continue our visits, child, so do not think all you have to do is dance the night away. But," Aunt Bea admitted with a sigh, "there will be fewer of them, and we will certainly not go out early."

Abby remembered that tomorrow was Jonathan's first day to join Thomas in the schoolroom, and she was determined to see him off herself. After all, she was spending little enough time with her brother these days.

"And tomorrow—" Lady Jeffrey interrupted Abby's thoughts "—I believe we should have a strategy meeting."

"What?" several voices asked at once.

"Well, with four of you attracting young men, it would be best not to mistake what gentleman is interested in what young lady... or vice versa."

Mary's heart sank. She needed no meeting to tell her that Lord Harrington was interested in Phoebe. But at least she had not had to stand along the wall unpartnered. She consoled herself with the thought that there were several men who had appeared interested this evening, even though they were not of the calibre of Lord Harrington. But none of them sparked any interest, and she closed her eyes, weariness stealing over her.

Abby watched Phoebe's face as she hummed a waltz. Her sister had enjoyed herself this evening, with good reason. And Abby was glad that Phoebe was happy. And that she was as big a success as she had thought she would be. But those two dances with Lord Norfolk worried her. The man was so much older than Phoebe... and so much more experienced. She must warn Phoebe once more about him, though she was afraid he had already cast a spell over her sister.

"YOU MUST BE SURE to follow all Mr. Brownlee's instructions, Jonathan," Abby said as she smoothed down her brother's shirt collar, all the while thinking what a handsome boy he was.

"Yes, Abby. Will Thomas be there?"

"Yes, of course, Jonathan. I told you you would be sharing his classroom."

"Then it will be all right. Thomas is a great gun."

"Just follow Mr. Brownlee's instructions," Abby said sternly, though Jonathan saw her lips curving up at the corners.

"I will, Abby."

"And stay with Crims. Do not run ahead."

"But, Abby, he walks too slowly."

"Jonathan..."

"All right."

Once Abby had seen her young brother and the servant out the door, she contemplated returning to bed. But there were several things she needed to discuss with Mrs. Healy and she should do so before the others were abroad, particularly her aunt. With a sigh, she started for the kitchen.

While most ladies in the ton would have sent for their housekeepers, Abby went to Mrs. Healy's room. It saved the housekeeper the trouble of climbing the stairs, a more difficult feat as she grew older, and it assured Abby uninterrupted time with her.

The two were going over the menus for the next few days when a loud roar with a definite French accent invaded their conversation.

"That's Monsieur Pierre!" Mrs. Healy exclaimed, starting up from her comfortable chair.

With a sense of foreboding, Abby quickly followed in the lady's footsteps. Surely her aunt could not be up already.

The diminutive Lady Jeffrey was standing in the centre of the kitchen, clutching a large canister of flour to her chest, resisting with every muscle the beanpole of a man who was tugging it away. As he pulled, he shouted admonitions at the woman who had invaded his territory.

"Aunt Bea!" Abby exclaimed, hurrying forward. "What are you doing?"

The servants fell back as soon as they realized who had followed Mrs. Healy into the kitchen. Only Monsieur Pierre remained in the centre. And while he stopped pulling on the canister, he refused to let go of it.

"Mademoiselle, please, not again. *Jamais!* She must never again come into my kitchen!"

"I shall, indeed! It is not *your* kitchen! It is—"

"Aunt Bea," Abby said again, this time pleadingly. "You must not upset Monsieur Pierre's routine. After all, we are sure to have many visitors today, and he must prepare his delicious pastries."

Retaining her hold on the flour, Lady Jeffrey assured her niece earnestly, "That is the very reason I must prepare some of my lemon cake. It is terribly important, my dear, that we have it ready for our guests."

Abby shuddered at the remembrance of the lemon cake the last time it was served. "But, Aunt—"

"No! It is necessary, Abby. And I shall not take long to make it if only this heathen will remove himself. He is refusing to let me bake it," Lady Jeffrey assured her niece self-righteously.

"But you 'ave promised, Mademoiselle! *Il faut qu'elle s'en aille!*"

Since neither combatant appeared willing to let go of the flour, private conversation with either of them was out of the question. Abby sought a compromise. "Dear Aunt, don't you remember our discussion? You promised that if we needed more lemon cake, you would give the recipe to Monsieur Pierre and he could prepare it along with his pastries."

"But he might not follow the recipe correctly."

"An excellent chef like Monsieur Pierre can follow any recipe, my love. Why don't we let him try it?"

"You prefer this...*cette horreur* to my *patisseries*?" the chef demanded in surprise.

Abby glared at the man while she spoke gently, "It is important to my aunt that we serve her special lemon cake, Monsieur Pierre. If you do not care to bake it, I'm sure Lady Jeffrey would be happy to do so."

"*Non! Non,* I will bake it, Mademoiselle."

"Thank you, Monsieur Pierre. Now, Aunt Bea, why don't you give Monsieur Pierre the flour, and we will go upstairs for breakfast," Abby said, her eyes flashing a signal to Mrs. Healy to ensure they would be served at once.

"All right, but first I must give Monsieur Pierre my recipe."

"Oh, yes, of course. Do you have it written down?"

"Of course not! It's secret!"

"Ah, well, perhaps if you wrote it down after breakfast, Monsieur Pierre would prepare it then."

"No. He must make it first before he makes his pastries, or he will forget."

Abby sighed. "All right, Aunt Bea. Mrs. Healy, could you fetch Aunt Bea some of the paper we were using, please?"

The housekeeper scurried to do as she was bidden, hoping to remove the lady from her kitchen before the French chef's notoriously short temper erupted again.

When Mrs. Healy returned with the paper, Lady Jeffrey retired to one corner of the kitchen, sitting at the long table where the servants took their meals, carefully writing the directions for her lemon cake, covering the paper with her left hand, as if all the servants were avidly anxious to steal her recipe.

When she handed it to the chef with the warning not to let anyone see it, he stared down his Gallic nose at her in disbelief. "*Madame,* no one would 'ave—"

"Thank you, Monsieur Pierre," Abby interrupted, afraid he might say something that would upset her aunt. "We will retire to the dining-room and have our breakfast."

Without another word, she led her aunt up the narrow stairs to the dining-room.

Lady Jeffrey protested even as she followed her niece. "Abby, I should have explained the recipe to him. He might not understand how—"

"Aunt Bea, I'm sure the man will do almost as good a job as you. But you must not slave for us. You have already done too much. We will never be able to thank you."

"Pshaw, child. It is nothing," Lady Jeffrey said warmly. "Why, I was going into a decline, sitting up north in the cold with nothing to do. It's I who should be thanking you."

Feeling guilty because her words had been an attempt to distract Lady Jeffrey from her recipe, Abby hugged the little lady as they reached the dining-room. "We will not quibble over who thanks whom, dear Aunt Bea, but we will be forever in your debt. I look forward to seeing my sisters happily settled.''

"And that is why we must have the lemon cake," Lady Jeffrey said with a firm nod.

Abby almost groaned that her aunt had not forgotten her famous recipe, but the significance of her aunt's words suddenly struck her.

Healy entered right behind them with several servants bearing trays, and the two ladies suspended their conversation to take their seats and be served.

Biting her lip in impatience, Abby waited until all but Healy had descended the stairs again. "It is all right, Healy. We will manage now. I know you have many chores."

The butler gave a stately nod and exited also, and Abby turned to her companion. "What did you mean when you said we needed the lemon cake? Why won't Monsieur Pierre's delicious pastries do?"

"Those things? All wind and no substance! No real man would prefer such a thing to my lemon cake. It has thickness, tastiness..."

"Oh," Abby sighed, relieved, "that is what you meant. That men prefer something substantial."

"Of course, Abby. That and the fact that it is magic."

CHAPTER SEVEN

ABBY, SIPPING TEA when her aunt spoke, almost choked. As she shakily lowered her cup to its saucer, Aunt Bea rose to beat her niece on the back.

"P-please, Aunt Bea, I'm all right."

"But you must be careful, my dear. Lady Sturdiman died when she choked on a piece of bread."

Abby ignored her aunt's warning and as Lady Jeffrey resumed her seat, she asked, "Aunt Bea, what did you say about the lemon cake?"

"I said it is filling...."

"No, what...what did you say about magic?"

"Well, I suppose I should not have said that, as it is not quite accurate." Abby breathed a sigh of relief, only to find herself gasping in alarm seconds later, when her aunt added, "I think it would be more accurate to call it a love potion."

"Aunt, you cannot be serious! There is no such thing."

"Oh, yes, there is. I once did a favour for an old gypsy and she gave me this recipe, only she told me to be careful because it is very powerful."

Biting her bottom lip, Abby said, "Aunt, surely you don't believe..."

"I've only used it twice. The first time I thought it was not working because nothing happened for my very dear friend, Mrs. Castle, a lovely widow. But Captain Worth did propose, only several weeks later. The second time, Mr.

Davidson was so overcome with passion, he fell to his knee right in the middle of my parlour to offer marriage to Miss Howe.''

"It must be coincidence, dear Aunt."

"No, I have decided it depends upon the gentleman's age and experience. Captain Worth had six-and-forty years under his cap and Mr. Davidson was a green youth. That is why I must be careful.''

Stunned by her aunt's revelations, Abby stared at her while her jumbled mind sorted through the implications of her aunt's tale. "And that is the secret that made you believe all of us would find husbands?''

"Of course, my dear," Lady Jeffrey said happily, patting her niece's hand before putting strawberry jam on her bread and eating it with enjoyment.

Abby opened her mouth several times but shut it before speaking. After all, what difference did it make if her aunt wanted to believe her cake had special powers? Her mind rejected the image of her aunt snatching the cake from Sir William or the scene in the kitchen with Monsieur Pierre. She would deal with such problems as they arose. The generosity of her aunt was worth those inconveniences.

"I'm afraid it will take several servings to Lord Harrington and Mr. Russell to bring them up to scratch,'' Lady Jeffrey remarked, before munching contentedly on her bread and jam.

In spite of herself, Abby could not help but ask, "Aunt, how do you...that is, which...how do you know to whom the gentleman will address his attentions?''

Aunt Bea frowned. "I have been studying that, Abby, and I admit to worrying whether others might reap benefits from my secret.''

"You mean you do not—"

"I shall ensure that all of you stay close to those who have been served."

"Oh, Aunt." Abby sighed.

"I do not think it will be such a problem, Abby, since the four of you are such pretty girls."

Abby, with visions of Phoebe surrounded by gentlemen on one knee while Mary and Kitty watched, shook her head to clear it. "There cannot really be any special powers in your cake, Aunt Bea, so, please, may we just forget all about this?" she pleaded before adding as an afterthought, "And I pray you will not discuss it with my sisters."

"But, Abby..."

"Dear Aunt Bea, we must not...we do not want to gain a reputation for being odd."

"But I may serve my cake to our visitors?"

Abby looked into her aunt's anxious eyes and her heart sank. She could not deny this woman, who was giving them so much, the right to indulge in a harmless act such as serving her lemon cake. "All right, you may serve your cake. But no more disturbing Monsieur Pierre in the kitchen. He will prepare it for you. And you mustn't snatch it away from our guests."

Lady Jeffrey muttered under her breath, but Abby did not ask her to repeat her words. She thought it better not to know what she had said. "I believe I will retire for a while, Aunt. Our late-evening revelries have taken their toll." She excused herself and went to her room, thinking longingly of the simplicity of their days in the country.

KITTY PACED the generous confines of the front parlour, the skirt of her blue serge walking dress swishing against the furniture. Her golden ringlets bobbed with every step, accentuating her emotions. She had risen early, at least early enough to be before her sisters, she thought, unaware of Abby's breakfast with her aunt.

There was purpose in her early descent. She had written a note to Peter and convinced one of the footmen, who was partial to young ladies with golden curls, to deliver it. She expected Peter to appear on her doorstep at the earliest opportunity. Her notes had always occasioned such a response in the past.

An hour later, Mary discovered her sister staring rigidly out the bow window of the parlour.

"Good morning, Kitty. You must have arisen early."

"Yes."

Mary looked at her sister's unyielding back and said, "Is something amiss, Kitty?"

That young lady whirled around, her eyes flashing fire. "Amiss? Why should anything be amiss?"

"You just seemed disturbed," Mary said carefully.

"Just because the man who swore he loved me did not even appear at the ball last night, after I promised him two dances, and did not bother to let me know he would not be there. And this morning," she continued, too enraged to be careful, "when I sent him a note demanding an explanation, he does not even answer that! Why should I be disturbed, I ask you?"

"You wrote Peter a note? Does Abby know?"

"Oh, don't be a tattle-tale, Mary. I wanted to know what could have kept him away. He *knew* I was counting on him to support me at my first ball."

"But you should not have—"

"You are such a prim and proper miss, you will never get a husband!" Kitty snarled in her rage.

Abby, entering upon her words, would have preferred to retreat once more. But she squared her shoulders and quietly asked the reason for Kitty's words.

Both of her sisters jumped, unaware of her arrival until she spoke. Then both rushed to explain.

"She did not mean—" Mary said.

"I did not intend to—" Kitty said at the same time.

"Kitty may explain," Abby said calmly as she sat down on the sofa.

"I . . . Mary said I should not have, but I sent a note to Peter." Watching her sister's lips firm, she hurried on, "I had to know what kept him from me last evening, Abby. Perhaps something terrible has occurred, because he did not answer my note, either."

"You should not have sent a note to Peter, but I'm sure he is all right. Promise me you will not do so again, Kitty."

"All right, but I don't see how I am supposed to know he is all right if I do not do so." '

"You would have heard if anything had happened. Ladies are not supposed to know where their men acquaintances are every moment of the day, my dear."

"Why not?"

"Because . . . I suppose they do not want us to know."

Lady Jeffrey entered the room. "Sir William and Lord Abbott have just arrived. I heard Healy admit them."

Kitty charged to the door, only to have her way blocked by Abby. "Dear, you must see Peter here, with all of us, and you must remember to not catechize him."

Kitty set her lips mulishly and retired to the sofa beside Mary, and Abby and Lady Jeffrey settled themselves to receive guests.

When Healy escorted the two gentlemen into the parlour, Abby nodded at his questioning look for refreshments to be served and hoped her aunt's lemon cake would not be ready.

The gentlemen greeted the ladies, though Sir William's face fell when he realized Phoebe was not among them.

Peter went immediately to Kitty's side, but she stared straight ahead and ignored him. Lady Jeffrey, unaware of the conversation which had preceded her entry, said, "We missed the two of you at Lady Mayberry's ball last evening, though the girls were besieged by young gentlemen."

Everyone tried to ignore the whispering going on between Kitty and Peter, and Sir William explained, "We intended to appear, but word came of a fight just a few miles south of London and Peter and I decided to go. After all, there are balls every night of the season, but only a few fights. The bruiser I backed won in the fourth round," he added proudly.

"But, Kitty—" Peter called out as that young lady rose from the sofa and stalked out of the room.

He rose to follow but was forestalled by Abby. "Peter, how are you enjoying London?"

"What?" he asked in confusion.

"I asked how you are enjoying London." When he showed no comprehension, she added gently, "You must give Kitty time to overcome her disappointment. I will apologize for her behaviour, but I know as an old friend, you will forgive her."

"Yes, of course, but I had no idea . . . Willie said it was done all the time."

"Of course, gentlemen do attend these . . . events, but I believe Kitty was counting on your presence to ease her debut into Society."

"Oh, lord, she will never forgive me."

"I'm sure she will, Peter," Mary protested. "You know she has a quick temper, but it never lasts."

Healy entered the parlour with several footmen bearing trays. Abby said, "Sit down and have some refreshment, Peter. It will make you feel better."

"Is Miss Phoebe not going to join us?" Sir William asked.

"No. You'll do better with Mary," Lady Jeffrey said absently, her eyes searching the trays for her lemon cake.

While Mary cringed in embarrassment, Abby said swiftly, "Aunt Bea means Phoebe is not an early riser. Mary is more conversable at this time of day. Are you at your best early in the morning, Sir William?"

"Lord, no. But we gentlemen cannot be lying in bed all day, you know. We have important things to take care of."

"I'm sure you must. What are your interests, Sir William?" Abby asked, flashing an importuning look at her sister.

"Well, I'm fond of horses. Have a nice stable in the country."

"Do you visit it often?" Mary asked faintly, wishing he would consider a visit in the near future.

"During the summer, you know, when the Town is thin of company. But I don't leave during the Season. Too much going on."

"I see. Do you not find the rush of the Season tiring?" Abby asked.

Sir William was as distracted by the refreshments as Lady Jeffrey. When she placed a large slice of her lemon cake on a plate, he ignored Abby's question and rushed forward. "I'll take that for you, Lady Jeffrey. Am I allowed to have a piece today?" he asked as he remembered his last attempt to taste the thick, lumpy cake.

"Of course you are, dear boy. I cut that piece specially for you. And Lord Abbott, here is yours."

Peter took his plate and cup of tea and sat down on the sofa next to Mary. After several minutes, she nudged him and said, "Are you not hungry, Peter?"

"What?"

"You have not even tasted your tea or the cake."

"Oh. Mary, what am I to do? Kitty has never refused to speak to me before."

"That is not true, Peter. Don't you remember the time you told her father that she had been throwing rocks at you?"

He laughed. "Lord, I had forgotten about that. She was quite furious, wasn't she?" His smile faded. "But that was a long time ago."

"Peter, you and Kitty have cared about each other for a long time. I can't believe she would throw it all away because of one night's disappointment. Send her flowers and a nice apology, and I believe she will speak to you when next she sees you."

"Thank you, Mary," Peter said warmly, smiling his thanks. Then he picked up his fork and tasted the cake he had been served.

Lady Jeffrey, seeing the warmth of his smile to Mary, wondered if the boy had changed his interest. As she watched him eat the cake, she hoped she had not made a mistake serving it to him with Kitty not present. She intended Sir William, not Lord Abbott, for Mary.

GILES RUSSELL wearily rubbed his eyes before bending back over the papers on his desk. How unfashionable he had become, done in by one night's late revelries. As a young man, he had never gone to bed until the wee hours of the morning. But then, of course, he had never risen as early as he was used to doing these days. Whatever his evening entertainments, he still had quite a bit of work to get through.

As he settled back into his papers, he was disturbed by a knock. His butler opened the door. "You have a visitor, Mr. Russell. It is Lord Norfolk."

"Send him in, Bates."

Though he had seldom had contact with most of the ton during the past years, he had frequent business dealings with Lord Norfolk and had come to count him as a friend. He rose as the distinguished man was shown into his office.

"Welcome, Jason. To what do I owe the honour of this visit?"

Lord Norfolk, forty-four and experienced in both social and business dealings, greeted his friend and settled in a chair before he attempted to answer that question. "This is a social call, my dear Giles, not business."

"Social?"

"Yes. Is it not strange that I, who have been so active in the social scene in London, should come to you, one who has hidden from Society, for assistance in a social matter?"

"I do find it quite strange, particularly in someone as astute as you. You should know I cannot assist you socially."

"Ah, but that is where you are wrong, my dear boy. It seems you have gained a certain familiarity with the lovely Milhouse ladies. And, since I have some interest there, I thought to better inform myself about the family."

"The lovely Phoebe, I gather?"

"You have no intentions there, yourself, do you?" Lord Norfolk asked, frowning.

"None whatsoever. Though I cannot answer for my cousin."

"Lord Harrington? Would that be a problem?"

"My loyalties would always lie with Richard. But that doesn't mean I could not give you some general information about the ladies."

"Ah, good. Who are they and what are their circumstances?"

Mr. Russell spent the next few minutes giving his friend what information he had, which was little enough, before asking, "Are you serious in your intentions?"

"You sound like the girl's guardian," Lord Norfolk remarked with a lazy smile.

Giles returned that smile, saying, "Not at all. I thought I should ascertain how stiff Richard's competition will be if he has an interest in that quarter."

"Did I hear my name?" Lord Harrington asked as he entered the library. "Good day, Lord Norfolk. I hope I do not intrude, Giles?"

"Of course not, Richard. Jason and I were just... discussing mutual acquaintances."

"Anyone I know?"

Giles hesitated, unsure how his cousin felt, but Lord Norfolk had no such qualms.

"Actually, yes. We were discussing the Milhouse ladies."

"Ah. Charming family. They are all quite beautiful, though, of course, Miss Phoebe is the diamond of them all."

"Yes, she is, isn't she?" Lord Norfolk agreed in a disinterested voice.

"They should all do well. My people are quite fond of them," Lord Harrington added.

"And do you have an interest in one of the lovely ladies?" Lord Norfolk probed.

"Me? Why, no. I have thought of taking a wife this Season, but I have set my sights on no one in particular." Lord Harrington covertly eyed his cousin, hoping for some sign of interest in the ladies under discussion, but he could detect nothing. Then he focussed on his cousin's guest.

"Do you have any interest in one of the Milhouse ladies?"

Lord Norfolk did not respond, coolly staring down the man's impertinence, but Mr. Russell came to his cousin's rescue. "Now, Jason, it is through Richard that any of us have met the ladies. I do not think it fair to conceal your interest."

With a shrug of his shoulders, Lord Norfolk said, "I do have some interest in Miss Phoebe Milhouse. As you say, she is a diamond of the first water, a rare beauty."

There was an awkward pause before Lord Norfolk rose to his feet and took his leave, promising to visit with Mr. Russell in the near future.

After his departure, Lord Harrington took the seat he had left, saying, "I am surprised that he is interested in taking a wife. It was my understanding that he led a rake's life, taking his pleasures where he pleased."

The tinge of disapproval in his cousin's voice amused Mr. Russell. "Any bachelor past the age of thirty tends to be stuck with that reputation, my friend. I will admit that Jason does not embrace celibacy, but he is not as bad as the scandal mongers make him out to be. And I think he would like an heir. He has built up an immense fortune from the small inheritance he received along with his title, though that is not widely known. I admire his courage and his intelligence."

"Then I'm not sure the lovely Phoebe will suit him. She has no notion of where to find the Orient."

"The oddity is that Miss Mary does, not that Miss Phoebe does not. Most of the lovelies thrust upon the ton for the Season are quite ignorant."

Lord Harrington shuddered before saying, "Pity. I had quite hoped Phoebe's loveliness would tempt you back into the social swim. No interest?"

"None whatsoever. I fear she would drive me insane within a fortnight. And before you make any additional plans, let me assure you Miss Kitty Milhouse is much too young."

"The thought never crossed my mind. But you have not mentioned Miss Mary, or Miss Milhouse."

"Must I specifically mention every young woman making her curtsy this season? They are all well and good, but I have no desire for a wife. You are the one who indicated some interest in that area."

"True. And the Milhouse ladies are charming, but I'm reserving my decision until I have surveyed the offerings this Season."

"Well, if you have any interest in Miss Phoebe, you had best hurry. I do not believe Norfolk will be long in making his choice."

WHEN SIR WILLIAM and Lord Abbott took their leave, Abby went upstairs to have a long talk with Kitty, leaving Mary and Lady Jeffrey doing needlework in the parlour. Only minutes later, their peace was again disturbed by Healy. "Miss Mary, a Mr. Morrison is below, asking for you."

Blushing slightly, Mary said, "Show him up, please, Healy, and bring refreshments."

"Who is this?" her aunt asked sharply.

"You met him last night, Aunt Bea. He is a distant connection to the Earl of Vye and is his secretary."

"Oh, yes. Pleasant enough, but rather boring."

As the door opened at that moment, Mary prayed their guest would not have heard her aunt's accurate assessment of him.

"Miss Mary, I hope you do not mind my calling, but I wanted to assure myself you took no harm from our strenuous evening."

"Come in, Mr. Morrison. Of course I do not mind your call. I am delighted you could spare us the time. I believe you met my aunt, Lady Jeffrey, last evening."

"Yes, of course. How are you, dear lady. You have such a charming family."

"Thank you. Please be seated. I'm sure Healy is bringing us some tea."

Mr. Morrison joined Mary on the sofa and began a monologue which covered minute details of the previous evening. She was relieved when Healy arrived with the tea tray.

Lady Jeffrey noted the presence of the lemon cake and eyed their visitor. Well, perhaps he was not what Mary wanted, but it could not hurt a young lady to receive several proposals. She sliced a large piece for the man and urged him to eat it.

"A special family recipe, Mr. Morrison. You must give me your opinion."

The man nibbled at the heavy cake, taking his hostess's request seriously. "I find it quite filling, Lady Jeffrey, with a refreshing lemon taste and . . . there seems to be a hint of cinnamon. Most interesting. I must take the recipe to my mother. She collects unusual recipes."

"I cannot share this recipe with anyone, sir, since it is a family secret, but please enjoy your cake."

"I can assure you I will. Any cake eaten in the presence of Miss Mary Milhouse can only be sweet to the taste."

Mary smiled faintly at such a fulsome compliment and hoped Mr. Morrison would soon take his leave. Just as with the lemon cake, a little of Mr. Morrison went a long way.

CHAPTER EIGHT

ABBY GREETED HER BROTHER anxiously when he arrived home from his first day with Mr. Russell's son and tutor. The house was certainly quieter through the day without a small boy's inquisitiveness upsetting the routine, but she missed him.

"Jonathan, how did your day go?"

"Hello, Abby. Fine. Mr. Brownlee knows a lot of interesting things. And Thomas and me have a great time."

"Thomas and I, dear."

"Yes, Abby. But after lessons this morning, we spent the afternoon in the park. Mr. Brownlee says it is important to educate the body as well as the mind. Isn't that wonderful, Abby? We ran races and rolled a hoop and everything."

"Yes, dear, that's wonderful." Abby wasn't sure about Mr. Brownlee's theory, but if it made Jonathan happy, she would not protest. "Your dinner's ready. Shall I sit and talk with you while you eat?"

"Oh, yes, please, Abby, if you have the time. I can tell you all about our lessons today. And Mr. Russell said he would take Thomas and me for a ride in his high-perch phaeton at the end of the week if we are very good."

"How kind of him. Did . . . do you see Mr. Russell during the day?"

"He ate with us. That's when he promised to take us for a ride. You don't suppose he'll forget, do you?" the little boy asked anxiously.

"No, I'm sure he'll remember if he promised. You didn't ask for the ride, did you?"

"No, Abby. I just told him how nice it was for Thomas to have a father who could take him for a ride."

"Oh, Jonathan."

"That's not asking, Abby, really."

"All right, Jonathan, but you must not do that again."

THAT EVENING, at the second ball of the Season, the debut of Miss Caroline Brent, a tall elegant redhead attracting a lot of attention, Miss Milhouse watched eagerly for the arrival of Mr. Russell. She wanted to express her gratitude to him for his kindnesses to her brother.

When he and Lord Harrington arrived, halfway through the evening, they surveyed the press of people. "The evening must be considered a success, I believe," Mr. Russell commented lazily.

"How true. The first real crush of the Season. I suspect it has something to do with the reputed beauty and fortune of the debutante."

"That's why you dragged me here, isn't it? My question is, are you considering Miss Brent for yourself or for me?"

"Ah, that's a secret I'm not yet ready to reveal."

"Well, I thought I would let you know that I do not care for redheads."

"Giles! Why could you not have told me earlier? We might have stayed at the club and enjoyed a hand of cards," Lord Harrington said with a sigh.

"It serves you right. I told you I was not interested in a wife."

"I know, but I cannot help but— Good evening, Mrs. Williamson. Yes, it is a lovely party."

Mr. Russell also greeted the dowager, then moved along to avoid a prolonged conversation. As he did so, Lord Harrington caught his arm. "I think you have made a conquest, whether or not you are interested. There is Miss Milhouse watching you."

Mr. Russell looked up, surprised. As his cousin had said, Miss Milhouse, standing a few feet away with several of her sisters, was watching him intently. He approached her reluctantly. He liked Miss Milhouse, but he had not intended to encourage her to think he might be romantically interested in her.

"Mr. Russell, I am so glad to have an opportunity to speak with you this evening."

Giles Russell almost turned tail at such an enthusiastic greeting. The woman must be expecting a proposal of marriage at the very least to greet him so.

"Miss Milhouse," he said in a withdrawn manner.

"I—I apologize, Mr. Russell," Abby said, embarrassed, her cheeks aflame. She had been so intent upon discussing her brother's education that she had not realized how forward she might seem. With a curtsy, she turned and walked away.

"Damn!" Mr. Russell muttered under his breath. He had not meant to give any indication he thought her behaviour inappropriate, but the stricken look in her eyes told him how ineffective he had been.

"Good evening, Miss Phoebe, Miss Mary, Lady Jeffrey," Lord Harrington said smoothly while he prompted his cousin with his elbow.

"Oh, good evening, ladies. It is a lovely ball, isn't it?"

"What did you do to upset Abby?" Lady Jeffrey demanded, ignoring the niceties.

"I assure you, madam..." Mr. Russell began stiffly.

"It is all right, Mr. Russell," Mary intervened. "Aunt Bea didn't realize Abby saw a friend across the room. She'll return in a moment, Aunt," Mary assured the older lady with a compelling look.

Lord Harrington stepped in to assist Mary in smoothing over the situation. "Dare I hope your dance card is not all filled, Miss Mary? Miss Phoebe?"

Phoebe joined the conversation when it centred on dancing. "Well, I can spare you one dance, Lord Harrington."

Mary stood quietly while Lord Harrington wrote his name on Phoebe's dance card, hoping he would not forget her once he had obtained the dance he really wanted. Mr. Russell, standing beside her, asked quietly, "May I also be allowed a dance, Miss Mary? I would like the opportunity to express my appreciation."

"Of course you may have a dance, Mr. Russell, but your gratitude is not necessary," she said coolly. "I was only trying to protect my sister's reputation."

Even though he was not forgiven, Mr. Russell signed her card for a country dance. As he finished, he found his cousin at his elbow. "Ah, my turn, I believe." He took the card and studied it carefully. "Yes, I believe I shall be greedy, Miss Mary, and take two dances if you do not object." Mary gave her agreement shakily, and Lord Harrington signed his name beside the seventh dance and then the eighth.

"But, Lord Harrington, I am not allowed to dance the waltz yet. Perhaps you would prefer to choose another partner."

"Nonsense. After dancing that country dance, I will feel the need of punch. I shall procure two cups and we will sit out the waltz and enjoy a chat."

Mary, who hated sitting in chairs watching the more experienced ladies whirl around the room, beamed up at him.

"Until the seventh dance, Miss Mary," Lord Harrington said, bowing over her hand before withdrawing.

As the two gentlemen strolled on, Lord Harrington muttered to his cousin, "What was that all about?"

"What are you talking about?"

"The contretemps with Miss Milhouse. You almost caused a rift between the Milhouses and us."

"I did not intend to do so. But she was staring at me so intently and then..." he paused to greet acquaintances and sign several other ladies' cards. All the while, however, his eyes searched for Miss Milhouse.

ABBY, HUMILIATED by her naïvety, retired to the cloakroom to repair a pretended rent in her petticoat. She had not realized how her behaviour would appear until she saw the look in Mr. Russell's eyes. She realized at once he thought she was setting her sights on him as a potential husband. She had never been so embarrassed in her life.

When she emerged half an hour later, her composure was firmly in place. She rejoined her aunt, who was sitting along the wall in one of the chairs provided for the chaperons.

Mr. Russell espied her reappearance from across the room where he was conversing with several friends. "Excuse me, gentlemen. I believe I must see someone."

Abby saw him approaching and quelled the desire to run away. She must do nothing to create a scene. Squeezing her hands tightly together, she stared straight ahead.

"Miss Milhouse, may I have this dance?" Mr. Russell requested as the orchestra signalled a new dance beginning.

Abby knew she could not refuse without causing rumours to fly about the room. There were too many people
within earshot. Without meeting his eyes, she said, "Yes,
of course, Mr. Russell."

"Or we could sit out this dance and talk, if you would
prefer."

"No, thank you, Mr. Russell. I would enjoy dancing."

Abby was dismayed to discover the dance was a waltz.
She had hoped for a vigorous country dance which would
leave no time for any talking. For several minutes, Mr.
Russell said nothing as he swept her around the room, and
Abby was left to enjoy the experience.

"May I offer my apologies, Miss Milhouse?" he finally
said quietly.

"That is not necessary, Mr. Russell. The fault was
mine."

"I cannot allow that, Miss Milhouse. I did not intend to
cause you distress."

"There is no more to be said, Mr. Russell."

They danced silently for several more minutes.

"Will you not tell me what you wished to say when we
first met?"

"It is of no moment, Mr. Russell."

He realized to pursue the subject now would only cause
her distress, but he wondered if he had misjudged the
young woman. After all, she had assured him she was not
looking for a husband. Perhaps it was conceited of him to
think she had selected him to fill that position.

They finished the dance in silence, Mr. Russell enjoying
the fragrant warmth of the young woman as well as her
graceful dancing.

When Abby settled back beside Lady Jeffrey after Mr.
Russell's departure, Lady Jeffrey leaned over. "He did not
offend you, did he?"

"No, of course not, Aunt Bea. Where is Phoebe?" Abby asked as she caught sight of both Kitty and Mary on the dance floor.

"She is dancing with Lord Norfolk," Aunt Bea said.

"But I do not see them on the dance floor, Aunt," Abby said sharply, though she kept her voice low.

"Perhaps they are having refreshments."

Abby nibbled on her lower lip, her mind completely distracted from her own problems by her concern for Phoebe. Lord Norfolk was too old and experienced for Phoebe, and she would prefer that her sister avoid him. She certainly didn't want her sister enjoying any private tête-à-tête with the man.

When the music ended, Phoebe arrived at her sister's side, her face flushed with an enchanting smile.

Lord Norfolk greeted Abby and Lady Jeffrey suavely before taking Phoebe's hand in his and placing a kiss upon it. "I shall see you tomorrow, Miss Phoebe."

"I shall look forward to it," Phoebe assured him.

Abby sat silently steaming, wanting to forbid the man their house. He would never do for Phoebe, and her mother had given her the task of seeing her sisters settled. She did not intend to fail her.

MARY ENJOYED her country dance with Lord Harrington, but it was the waltz she looked forward to. Even if she could have danced it, and of course she could not, she would have preferred talking to Lord Harrington. She wanted to hear all about his travels.

When he led her to the dining-room where refreshments were being served at small tables, Lord Harrington found a young lady truly interested in his adventures and knowledgeable about the countries he had visited.

"How do you know so much about foreign countries?"

Mary, remembering her aunt's strictures against appearing to be a bluestocking, fumbled for a response. "I—I like to read... when there are no dances, of course. My father had an extensive library and Abby had our man of business here in London send us new books when they came out because she knew I—we all enjoyed them."

"All of you?" Lord Harrington teased.

"Well, perhaps not Phoebe. She is so pretty, she seldom has time to read."

"I cannot imagine any gentleman of taste passing you by, Miss Mary. You combine beauty with intelligence."

Blushing a bright red, Mary said, "Thank you." She was thrilled by his words, though, of course, she knew her host was only following the rules of Society, offering compliments whether or not they were deserved.

"I also want to thank you for easing a difficult situation earlier with my cousin and Miss Milhouse. Do you know what went wrong?"

"No, sir, I do not. But I should not be thanked. I only acted to preserve Abby's reputation. And if your cousin is intent upon upsetting Abby, he will have me to deal with also," Mary said firmly.

Lord Harrington smiled. "I shall warn him, my dear, but I am quite sure he meant no harm to your sister. Giles is a kind man, but his social skills may be a little rusty. He was widowed nine years ago and retired from Society. This is the first time I have persuaded him to venture out among the ton in years."

"Did he not grow lonesome?"

"I believe he did, but he had Thomas and his business activities."

"What kind of business?"

"He has a large shipping concern. It gave him something upon which to concentrate after his loss."

"Poor man. I am sorry for him."

"If you can keep a secret, I will tell you that I am hopeful of finding him a wife this Season. He and Thomas need a woman in their lives."

"Have you discovered anyone suitable?" Mary asked hesitantly.

"Well, I thought perhaps Miss Phoebe with all her beauty might tempt him, but I do not believe he is interested in her."

"Oh."

"I'm sure it will require someone quite beautiful to lure him from his bachelor ways. I had thought Miss Brent might do the trick, but he told me he does not care for redheads."

"I thought perhaps *you* came this evening because you prefer redheads." Mary felt very daring making such a statement, but she thought it would be better if she knew there was no hope for her dreams.

"No. I am considering matrimony, but I have not yet met the woman who could keep my interest," Lord Harrington said, forgetting to whom he spoke. He found Mary so easy to talk to, he felt he was speaking to an old friend.

"Of course," she agreed, her heart sinking.

Something in her eyes must have reminded Lord Harrington that his partner was a green girl with whom he should have maintained the strictest formalities.

"My apologies, Miss Mary, I forgot myself. You are such an easy conversationalist, I did not—"

"It is of no matter, Lord Harrington. I am flattered by your confidence in me, and I promise I shall not repeat anything you have said."

He looked into her cool blue eyes and nodded his head. "I believe you. Thank you."

Mary stared into his eyes, which were green with flecks of gold, and wished she could always do so, but a movement near her brought her back to earth. "I believe the waltz is completed, Lord Harrington. It is the most delightful waltz I have yet to experience."

"It is I who should say that, Miss Mary. Only wait until you have been sanctioned to dance the waltz, and I will show you an even greater enjoyment," he assured her, startled to discover he was eager to do so. Lifting her small hand to his lips, he gently saluted it before assisting her from her chair and leading her back to her aunt.

WHEN THE MILHOUSES and Lady Jeffrey finally took their leave, all were exhausted. Even Kitty, with the energy of the young, had nothing to say. It had been a disappointing evening for her. Peter had warned her this time that he would not be in attendance. It seemed Sir William wanted to show him a gaming hell said to be all the rage. She had gone from partner to partner, all admiring and flattering, but they were not Peter. What was she to do?

Abby needed to question Phoebe again about Lord Norfolk, but she was too disheartened to do so this evening. Her embarrassment with Mr. Russell overshadowed the entire evening. She would deal with Phoebe tomorrow. And she wanted to talk to Mary about Mr. Morrison. That man had dropped some strong hints about his intentions toward Mary when she had met him this evening. He was not particularly appealing, but perhaps Mary felt differently. Ah, well, tomorrow was another day. And she prayed it would be a better one.

ABBY ROSE the next morning later than she had intended.
Jonathan would have already left for his tutoring at Mr.
Russell's. She wondered if she should halt their arrange-
ment. Though she had made arrangements to pay Mr.
Brownlee, she still felt she was imposing upon a man who
clearly did not want any closer acquaintance with her. For
Jonathan's sake, she decided to let it continue for a while.
She had too many other pressing matters with which to
deal.

With a stretch and a yawn, she reached out and pulled
the bell rope for Alice, her maid, then snuggled back under the covers to wait for a pot of tea. She felt uncommonly lazy this morning. She ruefully laughed to herself.
It was not laziness but reluctance to face all the problems
of the day. She must talk to Phoebe about Lord Norfolk,
Mary about Mr. Morrison, and it wouldn't hurt to have a
chat with Kitty. She seemed unhappy last night.

It must be a shock to poor Kitty to discover that Peter
was not willing to be at her beck and call in London. Always before, he had been eager to serve, waiting only for
her word. Unfortunately, Abby felt sure she had been
proven right. Kitty needed to look elsewhere for a mate. It
was too bad, too, since Peter's father's lands marched with
their own.

Alice arrived with the tea tray, and her cheerful chatter,
along with the steaming hot tea, raised Abby's spirits. She
set aside her empty tray and slid from the bed to dress with
a renewed spirit. She chose a rosy-pink morning dress with
white lace trim at the neck and long sleeves, the skirt fall-
ing from under her bust. It delineated her slender curves
and put colour into her pale cheeks. She drew her silvery
blond hair up into a simple knot on the top of her head.
With a final glance in her looking-glass, she was ready to
face the day.

Before she could reach the door, however, it was pushed open by an excited Aunt Bea. "Abby! Abby, I told you it worked. You didn't believe me, but I told you. Only, they weren't supposed to eat any. But don't be harsh on them. Everything will be all right. But it is proof, you see! After all, I was right."

"Aunt Bea, please calm yourself. I do not know what you are talking about."

"The cake, Abby, the cake!"

"Abby, Aunt Bea? Is everything all right? I heard shouting," Mary asked as she entered the open door.

"Oh, Aunt Bea." Abby sighed. "Yes, Mary, everything's all right. Aunt Bea just...uh, well, perhaps we had better go down to the breakfast room. Are Kitty and Phoebe up yet?"

"No, I don't believe so. Do you want me to call them?" Mary asked.

"No! No, I don't want them awakened. Let's go and have breakfast together."

The three women descended the stairs silently, but Lady Jeffrey's chin was in the air and her face wore a conquering smile.

After Healy had served them their breakfast, Abby dismissed him and turned to her aunt.

"Now, Aunt Bea, what were you telling me about the cake?"

"What cake?" Mary asked.

"My lemon cake. It is a love potion, dear," Lady Jeffrey said kindly, ignoring her niece's gasp of surprise. "I went down to the kitchen this morning to check on our supply of lemon cake—"

"Aunt, you were not supposed to interfere with Monsieur Pierre again. You promised." Abby interrupted.

"I did not promise not to go to the kitchens. I only promised not to cook the lemon cake myself anymore. Anyway, I went down to the kitchen and everyone was busy. Since I know you don't like me to disturb anyone down there," she said self-righteously, "I decided to look in the pantry to see if there was plenty of lemon cake. You'll never guess what I saw there!"

"No, I'm sure we won't," Abby said faintly.

"Rose was being kissed by a young man!"

"Rose?" Mary asked. "Our Rose?"

"Who else's Rose would it be in our pantry, I'd like to know?" Lady Jeffrey asked rhetorically. "Well, I put a stop to that at once, you may be sure. But then it occurred to me to ask if the man had eaten any lemon cake. They finally confessed that he had yesterday afternoon. Well, I knew at once why he was kissing Rose!" She smiled in triumph. "You see, Abby, I was right!"

Abby groaned silently. "Aunt, there is nothing to prove the two are connected, the kissing and the cake."

"Abby, how can you say that! The man is Lord Harrington's valet, Johnson. He had never met Rose until their return two weeks ago. And he had no intention of marrying anyone, he told me, but Rose just cast a spell on him. Those are his very words!"

"Are you saying he and Rose intend to marry?"

"Well, I don't rightly know that. He couldn't unless Lord Harrington agreed, could he? Or he might lose his position."

Abby rubbed her forehead and wished she had stayed in bed as her first inclination had told her to do. "Aunt, you didn't . . . surely you didn't say anything to the servants about your belief that the cake is magical?"

"Well, of course I did. It wasn't fair not to."

"Oh, dear," Abby said softly. The network of gossip-mongers among the ton had its base in the servants' rank. In no time at all, that information would have circulated throughout London.

"Abby, surely it isn't true...is it?" Mary asked with just a tinge of hope in her words.

"No, of course not, Mary," Abby assured her sister. "It is simply a coincidence. And if anyone asks you about it, you must deny such a thing at once."

"Why, Abigail Milhouse! How can you deny it? Haven't I just shown you it's true?" Lady Jeffrey demanded indignantly.

"Darling Aunt Bea, all you have shown me is a coincidence. Please, please do not tell anyone that your lemon cake is responsible for...for this romance!"

"I don't see why not! Just because you don't believe in my lemon cake doesn't mean—"

"Aunt Bea," Abby said desperately, "You haven't thought. If the ton hears about your lemon cake, half of them will beat a track to the door hoping to discover your recipe, and the other half will dismiss us as insane."

CHAPTER NINE

FOR ALMOST A WEEK, Abby thought they had escaped the notice of the ton. They appeared nightly at the various entertainments, but there was no undue speculation or intense regard from their compatriots. Phoebe, of course, always had her dance card filled minutes after entering, and the other girls seldom sat out dances. Peter began attending the evening entertainments occasionally, but Kitty frequently gave him the cold shoulder. Mr. Morrison always appeared at Mary's side, devoting himself to her comfort. And Abby maintained her watch over her sisters.

Lord Norfolk appeared at whatever party they chose, but at least he did not make a cake of himself over Phoebe. Abby still did not want her sister to become attached to the man, although there was nothing in his behaviour to which she could object.

Abby contemplated their situation as she lingered over breakfast. She had avoided Mr. Russell since her embarrassment, but that had not been difficult. Though Lord Harrington appeared at some of the entertainments, he was not accompanied by his cousin. Abby realized Mary was as infatuated as ever by Lord Harrington, but she had had a most satisfactory talk with her sister about Mr. Morrison.

When she pointed out the hints Mr. Morrison had been making, Mary reacted calmly.

"Yes, I am aware of his interest, Abby."

"But what is your desire in this, Mary? You know I would never push you into an unwanted marriage, but neither do I want you to dwindle away into an old maid."

"Neither do I," Mary said quietly. "I want to have children, to have a family. I really have no objection to Mr. Morrison. He is an honest man and seems to care for me."

"You want me to accept him? There might be others who—"

"No. We both know that—" Mary paused to swallow a lump in her throat "—that Lord Harrington has no interest in me. And I will outgrow my silliness. But if I cannot . . . I must marry somewhere, and Mr. Morrison seems inclined to take me."

"Oh, Mary." Abby sighed as she gathered her sister to her in a hug. "I do so want you to be happy."

"And so I shall. And when I have half a dozen little ones in the nursery, you shall come to visit and share my happiness."

"Thank you, love. I shall certainly visit you as often as possible."

"What about Kitty and Phoebe?"

Abby sighed again. "I do not know. Though Phoebe's dance card is always filled, there have been no offers for her hand. I overheard her discouraging a most acceptable young man last evening. When I questioned her later, she assured me he would never do, but she could give me no reason."

"Perhaps she has lost her heart elsewhere."

"But to whom? She has given no indication."

Mary hesitated to name the gentleman she thought stirred her sister's heart because she already knew what Abby's reaction would be. "Abby, do you not think . . . that is, it seems to me that Lord Norfolk is most attentive."

"I know he is," Abby said with a hardened voice, "but he is a known rake and old enough to be her father, Mary. The man is four-and-forty! That is much too old for Phoebe."

Acquiescing, Mary asked, "And Kitty?"

"I fear I was right that she and Peter are not suited. They have been estranged ever since Peter's arrival in London. But Kitty shows no inclination toward any other gentlemen." Abby covered her face with her hands momentarily before looking soberly at Mary. "Sometimes I wonder if I made the right decision to bring us all to London. Though we can afford it, it is a considerable expense and nothing seems to be going as planned."

Mary patted her sister on the shoulder. "Never mind, Abby. At least you will have got me off your hands. And the other two are so pretty, you know they will eventually find husbands."

The two sisters sat in silence, their thoughts on the future, before Mary asked one more question. "What about yourself, Abby—have you found no one of interest?"

Abby looked at her sister with real surprise. "Why, Mary, I thought you realized... You have been listening to Aunt Bea much too long. There was no intent to find me a husband. You know that at my age I am considered on the shelf. No, after the three of you are settled, I shall return home with Jonathan and continue as before."

Healy entered to announce the arrival of Mrs. Brent and her daughter Caroline. Abby and Mary exchanged curious glances before Abby asked Healy to give them a moment to reach the parlour before showing the women in.

"Why have they come to call?" Mary whispered as she followed her sister. "We scarce know them."

"Well, we did attend their ball," Abby said, shuddering as she remembered that evening, "and we have sent them cards for our own ball next week."

However, when the ladies were shown in, the conversation did not deal with balls.

"How lovely to see you," Mrs. Brent gushed, while Caroline stared intently at her hostesses.

"It is most kind of you to call, Mrs. Brent, Miss Brent," Abby said.

"Why, we have intended to call this age, but our time is so limited during the Season. Caroline is such a success," the woman added, beaming at her daughter.

In all truth, she was correct, and both Abby and Mary acknowledged her words with smiles. There was an awkward silence before Abby said politely, "Your ball was most enjoyable, Mrs. Brent. And Miss Brent, you appeared to great advantage in your lovely gown."

"Thank you," Caroline said, staring down her nose at the two young women. She knew she appeared to advantage beside these two. Only their sister Phoebe cast her in the shade.

Healy entered at that moment with his minions carrying trays bearing tea and pastries. Abby was glad of the interruption. She dispensed the tea and Mary served it. When Healy dismissed the other servants and offered the tray of pastries himself, Mrs. Brent carefully inspected each item on the tray while the butler gravely awaited her choice. Something in her manner drew Abby's attention.

"Is there nothing there to your taste, Mrs. Brent?"

"Why...no, not really. I was hoping to sample your famous lemon cake, but I do not see any on the tray."

"Famous?" Abby asked lightly while she shook inside. "It is true my aunt is partial to lemon cake, but I cannot imagine it being famous. I find it rather unappealing."

"It has been highly recommended to me. Do you have no lemon cake today?"

Mary and Abby exchanged surreptitious glances before Abby looked enquiringly to Healy.

"Yes, Miss," he said before slipping from the room with the tray still in his hand.

"I have always been partial to the taste of lemon," Mrs. Brent said chattily. When no one responded to her statement, Mrs. Brent continued. "We are enjoying Caroline's Season so much. We expect her to make an excellent marriage."

"How nice," Abby said quietly.

"And how are your sisters enjoying the Season?"

Though Abby knew the woman was probing for information about possible suitors, she said noncommittally, "They are enjoying it very well, ma'am."

"Of course, my Caroline is not new to London. We reside here at least half the year. I'm sure it is more difficult for your sisters, having never been to London before."

"We have found it a most pleasant experience, Mrs. Brent, with both my sister and my aunt to guide us," Mary said firmly, resentful of the woman's words.

Healy entered with the tray refilled, but before he offered it to Mrs. Brent, he whispered to Abby, "Lord Harrington and Mr. Russell have come to call."

Though Abby would have preferred the departure of Mrs. Brent and her daughter before dealing with the new callers, she had no choice. "Please show them up, Healy. I will serve Mrs. Brent."

"Oh. There are other callers?" Mrs. Brent asked with intense interest.

"Yes. Lord Harrington and Mr. Russell have arrived. As you know, we are leasing Lord Harrington's house for the Season."

"Yes, it is charming," Mrs. Brent assured her hostess as she mentally estimated the cost of the decor. Her daughter's eyes were pinned on the door. She had hoped to catch the interest of Lord Harrington when he appeared at her ball, but he had not called.

Healy admitted the gentlemen and greetings were extended before Abby offered the gentlemen refreshments. Both accepted their cups of tea but refused any pastries.

Mrs. Brent leaned forward anxiously, "But surely, Lord Harrington, you are going to try some of our hostess's famous lemon cake? I am having some myself, and I find it delightful."

The two gentlemen exchanged glances before Lord Harrington said, "I have already tasted the lemon cake, Mrs. Brent. It is certainly, uh, tasty, but I find myself with no appetite this morning."

"Ah, perhaps you have been stricken by love," the woman teased coyly. "I have heard it destroys one's appetite."

Mary stared straight ahead, afraid to hear Lord Harrington's response. Since she already knew from his own lips that he was in search of a wife, she had been preparing herself each day to hear news of his engagement.

"I must disclaim any such thing, madam, though there are certainly many lovely young ladies to tempt any man," Lord Harrington said gallantly.

"And you, Mr. Russell," Mrs. Brent continued to dominate the conversation, "have you discovered that certain young woman to bring joy to your life?"

Mr. Russell found the conversation distasteful. He had hoped for a private conversation with Miss Milhouse. It was his only reason for venturing back out into Society, but as long as this woman remained, that was impossible. "No, Mrs. Brent, my son brings sufficient joy to my life."

"But surely, sir, you long for a woman's touch in your life, someone like my sweet Caroline, to soothe your brow and grace your table."

Though such blatant offering discomfited everyone else, including Caroline, Mrs. Brent waited for an answer.

"No, ma'am." Mr. Russell made no attempt to soften his response.

Abby sought desperately for a change of topic. "Have you visited the Elgin Marbles, Miss Brent?"

Caroline Brent stared at her hostess in surprise. "Why, no, I have not. I have no use for piles of rock. I prefer balls to museums."

"But the Elgin Marbles are more than—" Mary began before Miss Caroline Brent interrupted her dismissively.

"To me they are not. Have you visited the many shops? You can find any style bonnet or kind of lace in London. Is it not wonderful?"

"Yes, of course," Mary subsided, sipping her tea.

Healy entered once more. "Miss Milhouse, Lord Abbott and Sir William are below."

Abby groaned inwardly. "Show them up, please, Healy, and bring more refreshments."

Mr. Russell sat watching his hostess maintain her composure when she must be wishing the entire group at the ends of the earth. He, too, regretted the new arrivals, for they guaranteed no opportunity for a private visit.

Mrs. Brent congratulated herself on her forethought in visiting the Milhouses. Now there were four highly eligible young men to admire her Caroline in her pale blue morning dress that showed off her slender figure!

Sir William and Lord Abbott greeted everyone, but Peter scanned the room for Kitty, who had not yet appeared. And Abby crossed her fingers that Kitty would remain above stairs until after their callers had departed.

She should have known better, however. Immediately the thought crossed her mind, the door opened again to admit Lady Jeffrey and her two sisters.

Abby was unaware that at least one other person in the room shared her feelings. Mrs. Brent knew her daughter could hold her own in looks with Miss Milhouse and Miss Mary, but Miss Phoebe outshone Miss Brent in everyone's eyes, even her mother's.

"Good morning, everyone," Lady Jeffrey greeted the guests. "You must excuse Phoebe, Kitty and myself. We did not rise as early as usual after last evening."

Peter jumped up to offer Kitty a seat near him and she deigned to accept it, much to Abby's surprise. Sir William's attention centred on the tea tray, his sweet tooth demanding more lemon cake.

Once the new arrivals had been served and Healy sent for more tea, Abby encouraged her sisters with her eyes to initiate conversation with their neighbours. The group had grown too large for general conversation. But Mrs. Brent, separated from Lady Jeffrey by her daughter, Mr. Russell, Mary, Lord Harrington and Sir William, leaned forward and ignored the conversational offering of Phoebe on her right.

"Lady Jeffrey, I have been hearing wonderful things about your lemon cake."

Abby closed her eyes before jerking herself out of her self-pity and placing a pleasant smile on her face. But she needn't have worried. Aunt Bea had no intention of sharing her advantage with others, particularly not this woman.

"Really? Well, it has a certain taste, a change from those high-falutin' French pastries, you know. But it does not appeal to everyone."

Mrs. Brent refused to allow the subject to drop. "But I have heard it said that your lemon cake has ... certain powers."

She now had the attention of everyone, but Lady Jeffrey was made of sterner stuff. Taking advantage of the stage her guest had provided her, she said dramatically, "Yes, it does." Abby held her breath as all eyes were on Lady Jeffrey. "It can provide you with a figure like mine if you partake of too much," the rotund little lady said with a gleeful laugh that had most of the company joining in.

The laughter routed Mrs. Brent. She detested being the object of anyone's humour, so, in spite of the eligible bachelors available for her daughter's perusal, she rose majestically to her feet and pulled Miss Caroline Brent after her. "We must take our leave, Lady Jeffrey. Such a delightful visit. I am sure we shall see you all at some of the balls." Without saying so, she left the impression the Milhouses would be lucky to find themselves in such elevated company.

Abby overlooked the woman's cattiness, only grateful she was departing without further questions about Aunt Bea's lemon cake. But the woman's questions told Abby that the servants had spread the word, and she feared others might not be so easily routed.

She was distracted by Mr. Russell. "Miss Milhouse, I wondered if I might tempt you with a carriage drive in the Park. There are several things we should discuss about Jonathan's education."

Abby's eyes flashed to his at the mention of her brother, but they dropped just as quickly. She had no desire to be alone with Mr. Russell, but Jonathan's education and his happiness were of great concern to his sister. "That is very

kind of you, sir. Would you object to Mary accompanying us? She shares my concern for Jonathan."

Mr. Russell recognized her ploy for what it was but gave
no sign of his irritation in his response. "Of course not. I
shall be delighted to have the company of two beautiful
ladies."

Abby paid no attention to his complimentary response.
She was just relieved to avoid being alone with him.

"I shall return in an hour, if that is convenient for
you?" he asked.

"We shall not keep you waiting."

Mr. Russell indicated to his cousin, who was chatting
comfortably with Phoebe, that he was ready to depart and
the two gentlemen followed in Mrs. Brent's wake.

"INTERESTING, wouldn't you say?" Lord Harrington
commented as the two men strolled along the quiet London street.

"What?" Mr. Russell asked, snapped from his
thoughts.

"I said, it was interesting, the bit about the lemon cake."

"What about it?"

"Are you all right, Giles?" Lord Harrington asked in
concern. "Did you not notice the Brent woman's questions about the lemon cake?"

"Oh, yes. It was unusual. But women are always curious about recipes."

Lord Harrington frowned at his companion, wondering what had distracted him. Usually he could count on his
cousin to share his amusement at the foibles of Society.

"I hope you have no plans for this afternoon," Mr.
Russell said abruptly.

"Why, no, other than meeting a few friends at White's.
Why?"

"Because I need you to accompany me on a carriage ride. I wanted the opportunity to ensure Miss Milhouse does not . . . is not still embarrassed about the other evening, but she included her sister in the ride. I thought you might even up the numbers."

"Lord, Giles, I've used up all my knowledge concerning fashion and dancing this morning. I can't possibly sustain a conversation for an entire carriage ride."

"But I thought you found Miss Mary quite conversable. I know she is not as beautiful as the others, but I think she is charming."

"You are right. I thought you meant Miss Phoebe. I should be delighted to converse with Miss Mary Milhouse. She has proven to be most intelligent and a delight."

"Is she a potential mate? After all, the Season is only so long, dear cousin. You must narrow the field soon."

"I have nothing against her, but, after all—" Lord Harrington paused to puff out his chest and raise his nose before saying loftily "—I *am* the catch of the Season. I shall expect nothing less than a diamond of the first water!"

Mr. Russell chuckled, as his cousin had intended, before saying seriously, "But beauty fades, my friend, while intelligence charms anew each day."

"Sounds as if you are smitten with Miss Mary yourself. Never fear, I shall stand aside and selflessly allow you to follow your heart."

"For the last time, my heart is not the question!" Mr. Russell assured his cousin more heatedly than he had intended, surprising both of them.

"MARY, DEAR, I must ask a favour of you. I know you intended to walk to Hookam's Library with Kitty, but I need you to accompany me on a carriage ride."

Studying her sister's agitated manner, Mary had no hesitation in assuring her of her cooperation. "Of course, Abby. I will be glad to accompany you. Is something wrong?"

"No, of course not. Just . . . Mr. Russell invited me for a carriage ride to discuss Jonathan's education, and I thought you might care to share in that discussion. After all, you have been a true support to me in making decisions about Jonathan."

"Of course I would," Mary replied at once, concerned about her sister's unusual agitation.

"Good. He will return in an hour. I shall . . . I must go and change. No, I will wear this gown. No, I had better change. He will be here in an hour."

Mary stood and stared as her normally decisive sister hurried from the room. Even Phoebe, usually unaware of currents around her, asked, "What is the matter with Abby?"

"I am not sure," Mary replied, but her mind was considering the possibility that her sister was attracted to Mr. Russell. Once the idea entered her head, she thought it wonderful. And if she could further that potential romance, then she was determined to do so.

MARY WAS NOT the only one to think one of the participants might have some interest in the other. Lord Harrington, at first taken aback by his cousin's irritation, reviewed their conversation. He considered whether his cousin's real interest might be the younger sister, but he dismissed that at once, with a surprising feeling of relief, since he had been asked along to distract Miss Mary.

The more he considered the appropriateness of Miss Milhouse, the more pleased he was. His cousin had chosen a lovely young woman who would be a wonderful mother to Thomas. She was a much better choice than Miss Brent, who seemed to be similar to Miss Phoebe. He laughed to himself that his first intention had been to match Giles with Miss Phoebe. That would have been a disaster.

So, his cousin had made his choice. And he would do everything he could to further their romance. Giles deserved happiness, and Lord Harrington wanted to ensure he received it.

CHAPTER TEN

ABBY, AFTER CHASTISING herself severely for her panic over a simple carriage ride, entered the parlour dressed in a vibrant green walking dress which emphasized her eyes and pale gold hair. The black frogging on the shoulders gave it a military air which she hoped made her look less vulnerable than she was feeling.

"Oh, Abby, I am so glad you have not left," Phoebe called from the stairs, causing Abby to turn back and look up to where Phoebe was standing.

"Is something wrong?"

"Why, no, of course not. It is just that Aunt Bea is accompanying Kitty to the library this afternoon and S-Sir William requested that I ride in the Park with him. I felt sure you would not object since you know him, but I just wanted to make sure."

Abby frowned but could not put her finger on what disturbed her. "Of course not, as long as his groom accompanies you."

"Oh, Abby, don't be so old-fashioned. Grooms are not necessary in an open carriage."

"Perhaps not, but I prefer that his groom accompany you."

"Oh, all right!" Phoebe agreed with a flounce before turning back to her room.

Abby entered the parlour, still frowning.

"Phoebe is going to accompany Sir William?" Mary asked from her seat on the sofa. She looked up from her needlework with a grin. "I thought she did not care for him."

"I did not think so either. That is what worries me."

"Perhaps she has had a change of mind."

"It is possible, but I doubt it. Anyway, we will probably see her there."

Healy opened the parlour door to admit Mr. Russell, followed by Lord Harrington.

"Good afternoon, ladies," Mr. Russell said pleasantly. "I hope you do not mind that I invited my cousin to accompany us?"

Both young ladies assured him the inclusion of his cousin met with their approval, though, in truth, Abby was not happy. Lord Harrington's presence would offset Mary's role as duenna.

"It is a lovely day. Shall we be off?" Mr. Russell asked as he offered his arm to Abby. Reluctantly she placed her hand upon his arm and strolled from the room.

"Miss Mary?" Lord Harrington said, offering his arm to the younger girl. Mary was delighted both for herself and her sister. Though she had no hopes of marriage where Lord Harrington was concerned, she enjoyed his company immensely, and an entire afternoon of such pleasure was not to be scorned.

And if, as Mary hoped, Mr. Russell had serious intentions toward her sister, his providing an escort for herself was a good sign. So she could enjoy what the Fates had granted her and still be assisting Abby.

Mr. Russell had brought a spacious brougham elegantly fitted out with leather cushions. Because of the beauty of the weather, the top was lowered. Abby was assisted into the carriage by Mr. Russell, and she watched as

Mary followed suit. But instead of taking the seat next to her sister, Mary asked, "Would you object terribly if I ride with my back to the horses, Mr. Russell? I love to do so in such a carriage."

Abby bit her lip and made a note to talk to her sister later. Both Mr. Russell and Lord Harrington were quite pleased with Mary's ingenious question and assured her enthusiastically of their approval.

Mary avoided her sister's eyes and immediately began a conversation with Lord Harrington. She only hoped he would not think she was trying to entrap him by her forward behaviour.

Mr. Russell waited until they had pulled away from the house, his driver manoeuvring their way through the afternoon traffic, before he spoke.

"Miss Milhouse, I appreciate the opportunity to speak to you. You rejected my apology the other evening, and there has been a stiffness between us ever since. I feel at fault for what occurred and I must make my apologies to you."

"It was my thoughtlessness which caused the difficulty, Mr. Russell, so there is no apology needed on your part. I was eager to talk to you about Jonathan, but I did not think how my behaviour would appear to you or others."

"That was all? You wanted to discuss your brother?" Mr. Russell said in amazement before he realized he had embarrassed his companion again.

"Please...could we not return, now that...now that it is cleared up. There is no need to waste your afternoon."

"It would be most ungallant of me to agree with you, Miss Milhouse. And it would also be a lie," he said as he smiled down into her grey eyes. "Time spent in your sensible company is always enjoyable. And we have not discussed Jonathan, as of yet, either."

Abby ignored the twinge in her heart at the word "sensible" and immediately set out to be exactly that. "Yes. I was concerned about his pestering you for a ride in your carriage. Please do not let him place an imposition on your time, Mr. Russell. It is distressing that he should show such a want of conduct."

"Nonsense. Jonathan is a well-behaved child. I offered to take him along with Thomas. In truth, Thomas has more fun when he shares with Jonathan. I think our arrangement is working very well for me and Thomas. How do you feel about it?"

"Jonathan is happy, and that counts the highest with me, as long as he is not disturbing your routine. I understand you are very busy."

Mr. Russell shrugged, but before he knew it, he found himself telling his sympathetic listener about his wife's death, the second tragedy of his parents', and the desolate years following. It was a subject he had seldom discussed with anyone other than his cousin.

Lord Harrington and Miss Mary Milhouse chatted easily with each other, but both kept an eye on the couple opposite them. When they discovered their mutual interest, Lord Harrington could not resist asking, "Does your sister...that is, do you think she has any interest in my cousin?"

"I am not sure," Mary whispered. "She was disturbed by his invitation, but I am not sure if it is interest or concern over the earlier contretemps."

"I hope you do not mind my encouraging such an attachment. I think your sister would be perfect for Giles."

"Abby considers herself on the shelf, but I want her to be happy, to have her own family. If I can assist you in any way, please call on me. Unless, of course, Abby should indicate she has no interest."

"Wonderful. We shall . . ."

Lord Harrington never concluded his sentence because Abby, gazing at the passers-by as she and Mr. Russell talked, exclaimed in anger when she saw her sister Phoebe riding in a high-perch phaeton beside Lord Norfolk.

"What is the matter, Miss Milhouse?" Mr. Russell asked in surprise. He had been enjoying their coze and had hoped she had also.

"Pardon me, Mr. Russell, but my sister...that is, I was surprised to see my sister accompanied by Lord Norfolk, that is all. I apologize for interrupting you." Abby's eyes met Mary's, but she said nothing more. She was even more horrified to see Phoebe bat her eyes and smile at her companion in a completely infatuated manner—like a country miss, or worse.

"Lord Norfolk is a well-respected businessman whom I consider a friend," Mr. Russell said quietly.

"Can you deny he has a reputation as a rake?"

"Not necessarily warranted, my dear Miss Milhouse. After all, the ton is not always discriminating in their labels."

"His name has been linked to many ladies," Abby muttered stubbornly.

"All of them willing, I can assure you," Mr. Russell said in amusement.

Abby did not respond to his sally, changing the subject to the weather, but the mood of their party had changed and they returned home shortly thereafter.

As soon as the two young ladies entered the house, Abby demanded of Healy, "Has Miss Phoebe returned?"

"No, Miss Abby, she hasn't."

"Did Sir William call for her?"

Healy looked confused, scratching his almost bald head. "Well, now, I believe it was Lord Norfolk who called for Miss Phoebe. She said she was to accompany him on a drive in the Park."

"Thank you, Healy. When Miss Phoebe arrives, tell her I would like to see her in the parlour, please."

Mary followed her sister silently into the parlour. "What are you going to do?"

"I am going to chaperon my sister more closely from now on. I am afraid I took too much interest in other things and forgot my duty."

"Is he really terrible?" Mary asked with a frown.

"I suppose he is not a monster, but he is totally unsuited to Phoebe. And worst of all is that Phoebe intentionally lied to me."

Mary nodded solemnly. "Shall I go upstairs so you can talk to Phoebe alone?"

"No, please stay, dear Mary. Even though Phoebe is older than you, I know she will be swayed by our unity on this matter. And she must be made to understand we are only working for her happiness."

WHEN LORD NORFOLK looked up from Phoebe's incredibly blue eyes to catch a glimpse of Miss Milhouse's angry face as Mr. Russell's brougham passed by at a distance, he glanced back down at the enchanting fairy beside him and asked, "Did you inform your sister of my invitation, my sweet?"

With eyes like saucers, Phoebe smiled and said, "Yes, of course, Lord Norfolk. Whatever made you ask such a question?"

"Because we just passed your sister and she did not look best pleased."

"Abby? Here? Oh, no, I thought…that is, are there not other places for rides in London? Must everyone come here?"

"Why should she not come here?"

"Oh. Well, I . . . that is, perhaps I did not mention who my escort would be."

"Your sister allows you to accompany an unknown gentleman whenever it pleases you?" Though he spoke sternly, there was a quiver in his lips that spoke of his amusement. Phoebe, however, never saw that sign.

"No! Of course not! Only women of a . . . a lower order would do such a thing. She even insists the groom be in attendance . . . ah, that is, she requested . . ."

"I think, young lady, that your sister is going to be most angry with me, and it will be your fault. For the first time in years, I have attempted to behave with decorum, and you, a wide-eyed babe in the woods, have circumvented my efforts."

Phoebe hung her head and allowed a tear to slip down her cheek, a talent she had developed at an early age. A knowing finger tilted her beautiful face up and Lord Norfolk said, "Enough of your play-acting, young lady. A solution must be found for our difficulty."

Phoebe stared at the man in amazement. Her trick had never failed to win her desires since she had turned sixteen, except with Abby, of course. Her respect almost matched her infatuation for the man beside her. "But Abby will never allow me to be in your company again. Whatever will we do?"

"There is one solution if you care to consider it." He paused while Phoebe nodded vigorously. "Even though I am considerably older than you, and incredibly more experienced…if you feel you could place yourself in my care, I could offer for your hand in marriage." In spite of his self-proclaimed experience and age, Lord Norfolk found himself nervously awaiting her response. This china doll with her trusting blue eyes had stolen his heart, leaving him unsure of his reception.

Phoebe stared up at him, her eyes wide and her lips trembling with genuine feeling, not artifice. "Oh! Oh! Lord Norfolk...I...you..." She stopped, unable to continue, overcome by emotion. She had longed for this moment, finding Lord Norfolk the man she desired above all others. He cared for her needs, and he never made demands upon her that she could not fulfill. And she found him most handsome.

"It is all right, Miss Phoebe. I should not have importuned you before speaking with your sister. Of course, I will carry this no further since you do not—"

"But I do!" Phoebe exclaimed, afraid her opportunity would slip away if she waited for him to finish his statement. "I did not mean...it is my fondest wish to marry you, Lord Norfolk, if you do not think I am too young, or—" she sobbed suddenly, "—too s-stupid. I cannot discuss things like Mary or Abby, and I do not have Kitty's spirit. I thought you would not...that I would not be clever enough for you to..."

Wishing he had not broached the subject in such a public place when he was unable to console his little love and reassure her of his desire for her, Lord Norfolk crushed her hands in one of his large ones while the other controlled his horses. "You are perfect, my dear one, and you must never believe otherwise. I have desired to make you my wife since I first saw you."

"Oh, Lord Norfolk, you are so...I have longed to hear you say you cared. I am so happy!" Again tears fell from her eyes, but this time they were happy ones.

"That is my constant desire, sweet one. And could you bring yourself to call me Jason? I detest the formality of Lord Norfolk from you."

"Of course, dear Jason. But I must not in front of Abby, of course," she assured him solemnly.

"Until after our wedding, perhaps. Then your sister will have no control over your life."

That thought had never occurred to Phoebe. A dawning look of wonder appeared in her eyes. "You mean you will be the only one to say me nay?"

"Yes, but you may rest assured I shall not allow you to run roughshod over me, my child."

Phoebe dismissed such nonsense with a beaming smile. "I shall adore it, dear Jason."

"So shall I, my love, so shall I." And the hardened bachelor's heart was never to be the same.

WHEN PHOEBE and Lord Norfolk returned to the Milhouse establishment, Healy explained Abby's instructions, but Phoebe, believing a proposal would solve all problems, brushed aside Healy's offer to announce Lord Norfolk and led him to the parlour. Her confidence suffered a setback when she first encountered her sister's eyes, but Norfolk's presence lent her courage.

"Lord Norfolk has come to call, Abby," she said eagerly.

"Oh? Did you encounter him during your ride with Sir William?"

Phoebe looked doubtfully at her sister before turning to the man beside her. He came to her rescue at once.

"I beg your pardon, Miss Milhouse. I was unaware that Phoebe had not informed you of my invitation until after we encountered you in the Park."

"I see."

The coldness of her response and the presence of the others did not bode well for his proposal. Lord Norfolk hesitated a moment before saying, "I wonder if I might speak to you in private, Miss Milhouse, in your capacity of guardian to Miss Phoebe."

Abby nodded silently, dismissing both girls with her eyes. Once they had departed, she stiffened her back and said coolly, "Please be seated, Lord Norfolk."

He did so reluctantly. He was determined not to be intimidated by a young lady half his age, but, in spite of Phoebe's assurances, he knew himself to be at a disadvantage. "Miss Milhouse, I wanted to speak to you to ask for Miss Phoebe's hand in marriage. I can assure you she will be well provided for and will be treasured as my wife for as long as I live."

"I appreciate your offer for my sister, Lord Norfolk. You do her an honour. However, I do not feel you to be a suitable parti for my young and innocent sister," she informed him with emphasis.

"I know it was improper for me to do so, but I discussed my proposal with your sister, and she assured me of her great desire to accept."

"You are right, sir. It was improper of you. However, it is of no account. You see, Phoebe was left in my care by my mother, and until she reaches her majority, she may not marry without my approval."

Lord Norfolk controlled his rising anger with difficulty. It was absurd that his happiness rested in the hands of someone so young and inexperienced. "May I ask what are your objections, Miss Milhouse?"

"Certainly. You are what, one-and-forty?"

"Four-and-forty," he said with gritted teeth.

"Then, four-and-forty, more than twice Phoebe's age. And your past has been...less than exemplary, Lord Norfolk."

"I am a man, Miss Milhouse! Men must..." he began before the indelicacy of his remarks struck him.

"I have nothing against you personally, my lord," Abby said, her confidence shaken by his distress, "but I would wish for...for more for my sister. I want a husband for her who will love her completely. Someone who will not have a past to haunt him at every turn. Someone who will be beside her the whole of her life, my lord. Someone who will bring her joy."

Lord Norfolk's face grew stern at her words, but, in spite of feeling she might be right, he would not give up. "Miss Milhouse, I swear to you that I love your sister with all my heart. I never thought to...that is, I would protect her with my entire being. I cannot promise to live as long as she. It is not within my power to do so. But I swear I would do anything to protect Phoebe from pain."

The baring of his emotions touched Abby deeply. But she was so sure she was right, she could not give in now. "I appreciate what you seem to feel for my sister, my lord, but my mother left me responsible for Phoebe, and I cannot agree to your proposal." She paused before adding quietly, "And I must request that you not call upon my sister again."

"No! Miss Milhouse, you cannot—" he stopped when he read confirmation of his fears in her face. "Is there no man to advise you in these matters? It is absurd that you, as green as your sister, should make this decision. Have you no male relative to whom I could present my case?"

"No, my lord, there is no one. Nor would such a person be able to sway my decision. I am sorry, but I never approved of your courtship. Perhaps I was too green to know how to avoid such a confrontation. For that I apologize.''

"I cannot accept this! After all these years, to find someone like Phoebe, only to lose her to your unreasonable prejudices! I will not bow down to your decision!''

Abby rose and stared coldly at the man. "I am afraid you have no choice, my lord. Good day!''

Lord Norfolk knew he had exceeded good manners, but his heart was involved for the first time in years, and he did not know how to deal with such a phenomenon. "You have not heard the last of me, Miss Milhouse. I will not give up your sister so easily.'' With those words, he strode from the parlour, leaving a shaken Abby to fall back on to the sofa.

CHAPTER ELEVEN

As distressing as the interview with Lord Norfolk was for Abby, the one that followed with Phoebe was even more so. That young lady was not only ungrateful for her sister's care, she grew hysterical when told she was to accept no further invitations from Lord Norfolk.

"But Abby! You do not understand! I want to marry *him* and no other! Please, Abby..." With tears flowing down her pale cheeks, Phoebe wrenched Abby's heart, but she remained firm.

"I am sorry, my love, but he is too old for you. You must allow me to know best."

"What is all the caterwauling?" Aunt Bea asked, opening Phoebe's door.

Hoping to find an ally, Phoebe jumped from her bed where she had thrown herself and dashed round Abby to her aunt. "Oh, please, Aunt Bea! You must not let her ruin my life!"

"Ruin your life? What is this?"

"I have refused Lord Norfolk's proposal, Aunt Bea," Abby explained.

"What? You cannot be serious! What a catch you have made, Phoebe! He is quite rich and has been the despair of matchmaking mamas for many years."

"You see?" Phoebe said, swinging round to face her sister. "Aunt Bea thinks I have made a good match!"

"Phoebe, you are too young to understand. I only want your happiness."

"You have not given me happiness. You have ruined my life. I wish to die!" Phoebe again fell across her bed, sobbing hysterically.

Lady Jeffrey ignored the younger girl and took Abby by the arm to lead her from the room.

"Now what is this, Abby? You have rejected Lord Norfolk's suit?"

"Yes, I have, Aunt Bea. The man is a rake and is more than twice Phoebe's age. She is the talk of the Town. I want a better match for her."

"You could not ask for a richer husband than Lord Norfolk."

"Aunt Bea, I want Phoebe to be happy!" By now, tears were streaming down Abby's cheeks, too. Why was life so difficult?

"GILES, YOU MUST help me!" Lord Norfolk demanded as he entered Mr. Russell's library on the heels of the butler.

Startled from his thoughts, Giles rose to his feet. "Of course I will help you if I can, Jason. What is the matter?"

"It is that female! She is impossible!"

"What female? What is wrong?"

"Miss Milhouse!"

"Miss Milhouse? She is the female who has upset you?"

"Yes. She refused my offer for Phoebe's hand!"

Finally understanding his friend's distress, Giles guided him to a chair and resumed his own seat. "Did she give any reasons for her decision?"

"Yes, of course. She said I am too old for Phoebe...and she is right, of course, but I love her. And she loves me, Giles. She told me so."

"That is the only reason?"

"No. She mentioned my reputation with women."

"Ah. She said something about that before."

"Giles, you know I am an honourable man. But I have not lived the life of a monk! Why should I?"

"I am not criticizing you, my friend. Did you discuss it with Miss Milhouse?"

"How can I? She's a green girl. I cannot be explaining a man's needs! And she says there is no man in the family to whom I could talk! That is why I came to you. Could you not plead my case for me?"

"Me? I have only recently made my peace with her myself. I am not sure she will listen."

"But you will try?" As if hearing the earnestness in his voice, Lord Norfolk gave a rueful laugh. "Is it not amazing? These many years I have gone my own way, caring for no one, and suddenly my life is topsy-turvy because of one young lady. Would you have thought it possible, Giles?"

"It is always possible for us men to become fools over the fairer sex, Jason. But I will speak to Miss Milhouse on your behalf. You must be patient, however."

"But she has forbidden me to see Phoebe!"

"I will do my best, Jason. Perhaps Richard will help, also."

"But he may be interested in Phoebe himself."

"No, Jason," Giles assured his friend, trying to hold back a smile, "Richard is not interested in Miss Phoebe."

"Why not? She is beautiful!"

"Of course she is, but each man looks for different things in his bride. I can, of course, urge Richard's interest in her, if it pleases you," he teased.

"No! Just do what you can for me. I—I must think.... You will let me know?"

"At once."

"When will you see her?"

"I will attend the evening's entertainments until I discover Miss Milhouse and arrange to talk to her about your problem."

"Thank you, Giles. I cannot tell you how much I appreciate your assistance."

The door opened to admit Lord Harrington. "Hello again, Lord Norfolk. I am forever interrupting your tête-à-têtes with my cousin."

"No, it...it is of no matter. You will be in touch, Giles?" the man asked anxiously as he moved to the door.

"I promise, Jason."

"What was that all about?" Lord Harrington asked as he ambled over to a chair.

"What I tell you must not leave this room, but I believe you may be of assistance."

Lord Harrington sat up in his chair, his interest heightened. "You have my word."

"Norfolk has offered for Miss Phoebe, but Miss Milhouse has rejected his suit because of his age and reputation."

"Unexpected, but Miss Milhouse is most protective of her sisters."

"Yes, but Norfolk truly cares for Phoebe, and I believe he would take good care of her."

"Did he ask you to intercede for him?"

"Yes, and you can help him also."

"How?"

Mr. Russell paced the library floor, rubbing his chin as he thought. "You and Miss Mary Milhouse seem able to discuss many things. Could you recommend Lord Norfolk to her? If she is in favour of the marriage, perhaps it would sway Miss Milhouse."

"I will try, but..."

"That is all I ask, Richard. Truly, Norfolk is an honourable man, and Miss Phoebe has expressed a desire to accept his proposal."

"Very well. Shall I approach her this evening?"

"Yes. I wish we knew what entertainment they will be attending this evening. There are several, I believe."

Lord Harrington looked at his cousin strangely. "Have you been looking through the invitations?" His curiosity rose as Mr. Russell's cheeks flushed.

"I—I was considering going out this evening. I wondered what was offered, that is all."

"Of course. Well, I will look at them, also. Perhaps I can deduce what entertainment would be the most attractive to the ladies."

"You are certainly more experienced than I."

Lord Harrington left the library and went immediately to his room. After only several minutes there, he rang for his valet.

"Johnson, could you have a note delivered to Miss Mary Milhouse without her sister's knowledge?" he asked.

"Yes, Sir," the man assured him. "I'll just step round to the house and deliver it myself to Rose, Miss Mary's maid."

"Just be sure Miss Milhouse or her aunt does not see you, and . . . wait for an answer."

MARY WAS RESTING in her room, exhausted by Phoebe's hysterics, when Rose tiptoed in. "Miss Mary?"

Raising her head from the down pillow, Mary said, "Yes, Rose? Does Abby need me?"

"Oh, no, Miss Mary. Robert, that is, Mr. Johnson, brought a note for you."

"Mr. Johnson? Isn't he Lord Harrington's man?"

"Yes, Ma'am," Rose said with a blush.

"Where is the note?"

"Here. And I am to wait for an answer."

Mary's heart was aflutter at the thought of a letter from Lord Harrington. When she could still her fingers long enough to read the message, she frowned. "Prepare me a quill, Rose. I must write an answer." She knew they had originally planned to attend Mrs. Littlefield's musicale this evening. But she was not sure Abby would feel up to it after the to-do this afternoon.

Writing this information on the note, she refolded it and returned it to Rose, though she would have liked to keep her only note from Lord Harrington. "Please give this back to Johnson secretly, Rose. And thank you."

"Yes, Ma'am," Rose agreed, before hurrying from the room.

"I THINK WE WILL remain at home this evening, Mary. After my interview with Phoebe, I do not feel up to going out."

"But we have already sent our acceptances. Do you not think it will cause talk?"

Abby frowned, considering Mary's words, and then shrugged. "I suppose you are right. But I am sure Phoebe cannot be seen in public. Her eyes will remain red for hours, even could she find the energy to arise from her bed."

"We shall tell everyone she is not feeling well."

"Very well."

Mary felt guilty at urging her exhausted sister to go out. But she hoped to further a romance with Mr. Russell by doing so. Of course, she admitted to herself, she would enjoy seeing Lord Harrington, also. But she was acting in Abby's best interest.

IN SPITE OF her avowed selfless behaviour, it was for Lord Harrington that Mary watched at the musicale that evening, not Mr. Russell. Indeed, she was so intent upon searching for him, she almost ignored Mr. Morrison when he approached.

"Miss Mary, you are in fine frame this evening."

"Oh. Oh, thank you, Mr. Morrison. I am looking forward to the music this evening," she said, but her actions belied her words. She remained turned to the door, her eyes addressing each new arrival.

"You are expecting someone?" the man asked in irritation.

"Why, no. I am just curious to see who will be in attendance."

"Bound to be the same people as at all the other entertainments during the Season."

"I believe there were a number of other entertainments this evening, Mr. Morrison," Mary pointed out politely.

"Well, yes, but . . ."

Mary had no idea what else Mr. Morrison had to say about those in attendance as she spotted a tall, auburn-haired gentleman who commanded her attention.

"Miss Mary! You have not answered me."

With her eyes still on Lord Harrington, she said absent-mindedly, "Yes, Mr. Morrison? What was your question?"

"I asked—"

"Miss Mary. Have you been here long?" Lord Harrington asked as he reached Mary's side, and she never heard Mr. Morrison's question.

"No, not long, my lord. We arrived only a few minutes ago."

"Where is your sister?"

"Excuse me, Lord Harrington!" Mr. Morrison inserted heatedly. "I was conversing with Miss Mary."

"Oh. Pardon me—Morrison, isn't it? I am sorry to interrupt, but Miss Mary and I share a common concern about . . . about a friend."

"If I can be of assistance to you, Miss Mary," Mr. Morrison offered pompously. "After all, I am related to the Earl of Vye."

"Thank you, Mr. Morrison, but it is of a personal nature, and only Lord Harrington can assist me."

"I'm sure I—"

"If you will excuse us, Mr. Morrison, Miss Mary and I desire to stroll about the room," Lord Harrington cut in ruthlessly, impatient with the man's determination to remain beside Mary.

Disturbed by the hurt shown on his face, Mary patted Mr. Morrison's arm. "I beg your pardon, Mr. Morrison, but it truly is urgent."

"Very well. I will call on you on the morrow."

With a smile from Mary and a glower from Lord Harrington, Mr. Morrison moved away from them.

"Why do you tolerate him? The man is a bore!"

"Lord Harrington! There is nothing wrong with Mr. Morrison. And he has been quite pleasant to me."

"And why shouldn't he be? Never mind. I refuse to waste valuable time discussing that man. I must apologize for writing to you secretly. I know I should not have, but I needed to talk to you this evening. And I'm sure Giles wanted to talk to Miss Milhouse even before."

"Before what?"

"Ah, that is the crux of the matter. You see, Lord Norfolk visited Giles after he left your residence today and asked for our assistance."

Mary had been enjoying her time with Lord Harrington, but at the mention of Lord Norfolk as his reason for seeking her out, Mary's face closed like a wilting flower. "Please, Lord Harrington, I must not discuss—"

"Mary, listen to me." Though she was shocked at his informality, he seemed unaware of it. "You are all green girls. I know how difficult it must be for Miss Milhouse, but she has no man to advise her and—"

"My sister is intelligent and—"

"Of course she is. But you do not understand the ways of the ton."

"My sister has only Phoebe's best interests at heart. Phoebe has always been easily swayed. While she may feel herself in love with Lord Norfolk now, that is not to say she will feel the same way in a month."

"I cannot argue with Miss Phoebe's whimsical nature, Mary, but you must—"

The pair was brought to attention by the tuning of the pianoforte by the first performer and their hostess's calling of her guests to take their seats. Lord Harrington saw his cousin motioning to him across the room and he directed Mary towards him.

"Good evening, Miss Mary. Is Miss Milhouse here tonight also? I have not seen her since my arrival."

"Good evening, Mr. Russell. My sister is here. She was talking with Mrs. Whitehall earlier when I . . . before your arrival."

At that moment, Abby entered from the dining-room and all three moved as one to meet her. Mary and Lord Harrington only smiled in greeting, but Mr. Russell grasped her hand and said, "Good evening, Miss Milhouse. I am happy to see you. I began to think you were not here."

"I was...discussing recipes with Mrs. Whitehall," Abby said with a speaking look to her sister. "Was there something in particular you wanted to discuss with me?"

Mary held her breath, knowing Abby would take offence should Mr. Russell attempt to advise her about Phoebe. To her relief, Mr. Russell did no such thing.

"No. I only wanted to tell you how much I enjoyed our drive this afternoon. You are a very pleasant companion." The smile that removed the harshness from his features spread across his face.

Abby returned his warmth, her hand still held in his. "I enjoyed our ride, also, Mr. Russell."

"Perhaps you would care to drive out again tomorrow?"

"I am not sure...I may be needed at home."

"You must not sacrifice your happiness for your family too much, Miss Milhouse. I would suffer from it." The caress in his voice delighted all three of his listeners, though Abby only considered him to be friendly.

"I believe we must take our seats or be considered ill-mannered," Lord Harrington whispered.

Brought back to an awareness of their surroundings, Abby blushed and snatched her hand from Mr. Russell's. He imperturbably took her arm and escorted her to the back of the room, where a few seats remained. Lord Harrington and Mary followed. The two couples were forced to sit apart, and they were carefully observed by the rest of the audience.

A beanpole of a young lady dressed in an ill-chosen white gown took her seat at the pianoforte and began playing a ballad, while her sister, a copy of the musician, sang in a weak voice.

Lord Harrington leaned toward Mary to whisper. "May I take you for a drive tomorrow? I must have an opportunity to plead Lord Norfolk's case. I promised my cousin.''

Before Mary could answer, a heavy-set matron in front of them, who happened to be a particular friend of the performers' family, shushed him. Mary could barely restrain a smile at his embarrassment. She cast him a merry glance and then pointedly turned her attention to the programme.

In spite of his frustration, Lord Harrington was appreciative of his companion. While she might not be considered a diamond, Lord Harrington found Mary, with such variety and honesty in her reactions to life, infinitely more interesting than any of the celebrated beauties.

Mr. Russell cast sidelong glances at Miss Milhouse, his attention on her rather than the entertainment. Her silver-blond hair was elegantly arranged and she was wearing a silver evening gown with pink roses that enhanced her trim figure and made her eyes appear huge. Even more importantly, she was a charming companion. He looked forward to their outing tomorrow, when he would not be restrained by the horrendous performance occurring at the moment, forgetting that his true purpose was not enjoying Abby but swaying her decision about Lord Norfolk.

''PHOEBE? Are you all right?'' a voice whispered in the dark.

''Kitty?'' Phoebe asked hoarsely, her voice strained from her earlier bout of tears.

''Yes. Shall I light a candle?''

''Please.''

There were several noises as Kitty moved across the room in the dark. Finally, the shimmering light of a candle lit a small portion of the room, its circle growing ever closer as Kitty moved to the bed. She set the candle down on the bedside table and moved back across the room to fetch a tray.

"I brought us some chocolate to drink. Mrs. Healy fixed it herself. She said you did not eat your supper."

"Oh, Kitty, thank you so much."

The two young ladies huddled together on the big bed, sipping their chocolate in the deep shadows. "Do you love him?" Kitty finally whispered, as if she could not help herself.

Phoebe sighed and sipped her chocolate. Finally she said, "Yes. Yes, I love him. Lord Norfolk does not mind that I am not clever like you and Mary and Abby. He never wants to discuss things I do not understand. And he is fabulously wealthy!"

Kitty nodded her head, an enlarged shadow repeating her movement on the wall behind her. "Perhaps Abby will change her mind."

"I do not think so," Phoebe said with a sob. "She did not let you marry Peter."

"No. But she may have been right. Everything is different now that we are in London."

"You do not love Peter?"

"Of course I love him. I shall always love him," Kitty said mournfully. "But I know he does not love me."

"But Kitty, he must! He has always loved you!"

"It does not matter," she responded. "I shall marry someone else. I will not sit on the shelf."

"But who shall you marry?"

"I do not know. Perhaps Lord Baskin. You met him two nights ago," she added helpfully at Phoebe's bewildered stare.

"I did? I do not remember. I can only remember Lord Norfolk. Is he not handsome, Kitty?"

"Of course he—"

"What was that?" Phoebe gasped, her eyes growing large.

"Did you hear something?"

Kitty's question was answered by a scream from down below. Phoebe grabbed her sister's arms in a desperate clutch. "Kitty, what could it be?"

"I do not know, but we must investigate. Abby, Mary and Aunt Bea went to the musicale."

"But surely the servants..."

Pulling herself loose from her sister's grasp, Kitty picked up the candle and headed for the door. Rather than remain alone in the dark, Phoebe reluctantly followed her, clutching the sleeve of her sister's gown.

CHAPTER TWELVE

THE THREE WOMEN returning to Lord Harrington's town house that evening were in different frames of mind. Abby was dreamily content to think of her ride with Mr. Russell on the morrow, in spite of the difficulties she had faced that day.

Mary's enjoyment of tomorrow's plans was tempered by the knowledge that Lord Harrington sought her out to sway her opinion toward Lord Norfolk. Even worse was the fear that Mr. Russell would anger Abby and they would be estranged forever.

Lady Jeffrey, who should have been the most content of the three, found herself irritated by members of the ton who hinted for the recipe of her lemon cake. At first it had been enjoyable, fending off their advances. But she soon tired of their tricks. Were it not for her nieces, she would forget she had ever heard of the magical powers of her cake.

When their knock at the door brought no response, all three ladies were forced to bring their thoughts to the present moment.

"Where could Healy be?" Lady Jeffrey demanded wearily.

"Perhaps he fell asleep," Mary suggested. "I'll knock again." Before she could do so, however, footsteps were heard running to the door.

A young footman pulled open the door, and the three ladies entered.

"Where is Healy?" Abby asked.

"He be downstairs with Mrs. Healy," the footman panted.

"Is everything all right?"

"Yes'm, 'cept for the burglar."

"What?" both Lady Jeffrey and Abby asked at once.

"Mrs. Healy, she found a burglar in the pantry."

"Good heavens," Abby exclaimed as she turned and hurried down the hall to the stairs that led to the kitchens. There she discovered both her sisters, the Healys and all the other servants in the house.

"Whatever has happened?" Abby asked, going at once to Mrs. Healy's side.

That lady, usually rosy-cheeked, was white-faced and shaking, sitting in a chair, with her arm being patted comfortingly by her husband.

"Oh, Miss Abby, it gave me such a turn. There he was, this big, dark man. He just shoved me down and ran out that door," the lady said, pointing to the back entrance.

"Is everyone all right? Were you injured, Mrs. Healy?" Mary asked.

"Just a few bruises, Miss, where they shouldn't be mentioned. But it did give me a turn!"

"But what did he take? Was he someone who only needed food? Surely he had only to ask if he were starving?" Abby asked with a frown.

"That's right, Miss. We don't waste food, but we've many a time found an extra plate for a man down on his luck," Healy assured Abby.

"Then I do not understand. What was taken?"

"That's the strange thing, Miss Abby," Rose ventured. "I looked in the pantry, but the only thing bothered was the plate of Lady Jeffrey's lemon cake. The ham and chickens and Monsieur Pierre's pastries, the potatoes and other vegetables, all were left untouched. You'd think a hungry man would want something other than lemon cake."

Abby grew still and Mary's eyes rounded. Lady Jeffrey had no hesitation in expressing the others' thoughts. "Aha! You see, Abby, others believe even if you do not!"

The servants' questioning looks brought Abby into action. "Aunt Bea, we will discuss this abovestairs. The rest of you must return to your beds. I'm sure this will not happen again. A hungry man will not harm anyone."

"But Abby—"

"Later, please, Aunt Bea. Everyone is tired now."

While the servants were obeying Abby's orders, Mary led Lady Jeffrey and her sisters up to the parlour to await Abby. "Neither of you was hurt?" she asked Phoebe and Kitty.

"No, of course not," Kitty said.

"Only frightened," Phoebe murmured.

"But what did Aunt Bea mean?" Kitty demanded. "What is it that others believe?"

Before Lady Jeffrey could respond, as she seemed intent on doing, Mary said, "Abby will explain, I'm sure. We should wait for her."

Since Abby arrived at once, it required no strength of character to remain silent. Kitty demanded, "What did Aunt Bea mean, Abby?"

Abby wearily shook her head, as if to clear it, before turning to Kitty. "Aunt Bea believes her lemon cake had—has certain powers."

"It's a love potion. I proved it to Abby, but she still wouldn't believe me. Well, someone else does. They were after my lemon cake recipe."

"A love potion?"

"Certainly. That's why you have all been successful. I knew that all of you would find husbands once they had tasted my lemon cake."

"But none of us has found husbands," Kitty said, "except Phoebe, and Abby won't let her marry him!"

"Humph! Another who doesn't believe me! My own family! At least *someone* knows my cake has special powers."

"The question now is not whether any of us believes you, Aunt Bea, or whether or not the cake has supernatural powers. The question is what are we going to do about it now that others believe that your cake is . . . different."

"I shall keep the cake under lock and key, and make sure that dratted chef doesn't let the recipe get away from him!" Lady Jeffrey assured her niece dramatically.

"No, Aunt Bea. I think we must do just the opposite."

"What do you mean, Abby?" Mary asked.

"I think we must give the recipe to anyone who asks, as if it mattered not one whit."

"What?" Aunt Bea shrieked. "Well, I never! To think I would be betrayed by my own blood!"

"Darling Aunt Bea," Abby pleaded, putting her arm around the elderly lady, "it is the only way. Otherwise, we will be pestered for the rest of the Season. And any attachments would be suspect. Young men would be afraid to eat your lemon cake because of its purported powers, so it would be of no use to us anyway."

"Abby is right, Aunt Bea," Mary said quietly. "It will be impossible to show ourselves in the ton again if everyone believes we are hoarding such a secret."

"Well, I will not! It was my gift to you girls, to find you all husbands. You, too, Abby. I wanted you all to be

happy, just as I was. And now you will give that away!''
she protested fiercely.

All four girls surrounded their aunt, each trying to assure Aunt Bea of their appreciation. However, their efforts did not appease her.

"Why do we not go to bed now, and discuss this again
in the morning?'' Abby finally suggested, seeing the real
weariness evident on Lady Jeffrey's face.

By the time all the members of her family were tucked
up in their beds, Abby was exhausted. How she longed for
her quiet country life, she thought as she undressed. But
then she would not have met Mr. Russell. That thought
frightened Abby. She had not realized how much she enjoyed his company until that moment. It had been easy to
convince herself that it was only on Jonathan's behalf that
she spent time with Mr. Russell.

Had it been in her power, Abby would have moved the
entire household back home in that moment. The danger
of losing her heart to a man impossibly beyond her reach
had never really occurred to Abby, but now she knew it
could happen—if it had not already.

With a weary sigh, she settled back against her pillows.
Perhaps tomorrow sanity would return. Tonight she
wanted to shut her eyes to the madness which surrounded
her and forget she had ever left home.

"DID YOU SPEAK to Miss Mary Milhouse?'' Mr. Russell
asked Lord Harrington as they rode back to his home in
the carriage.

"Yes. She is a delight.''

"I meant about Norfolk's problem,'' Mr. Russell asked
with a grin.

"Oh. Yes, of course, though only for a moment. Mary
says Miss Phoebe changes her mind frequently.''

Mr. Russell frowned. "Well, I find that easy to believe. The girl does not appear to be highly intelligent."

"I asked Mary to accompany me tomorrow on a drive, and I will talk to her again, but she did not feel Miss Milhouse would change her mind easily."

"Mary? She gave you permission to address her so?"

Lord Harrington's cheeks flushed. "No, I just forgot for a moment. Miss Mary Milhouse is so conversable, it is as if I am talking to an old friend."

"That is not a bad quality in a wife," Mr. Russell suggested with a grin.

"No, it isn't, is it? Not that I am thinking along those lines," Lord Harrington hastily assured his cousin when he realized what he had said.

"Just don't forget Norfolk tomorrow when you are enjoying yourself. After all, I did promise."

"I do not think I am the only one who should take such advice to heart," Lord Harrington could not resist saying.

"Abby, you are right."

Abby had not expected such easy capitulation from her aunt.

"You mean you will give the recipe to the ton?" she asked in amazement as she sat down at the breakfast table.

"Yes. I thought about what you said, and it is true that the men will refuse to eat any if they believe it has magical powers. So it would be useless. But if we give it to everyone, they will simply eat it because of its good taste. But I shall leave out one special ingredient. Then others will not think it special but it will still work for us."

"If you are sure no one will realize what you have done. We must convince them of its harmlessness," Abby said worriedly.

"I am sure," Aunt Bea said. "And it serves those noseyparkers right," she muttered under her breath.

"Why do you not write a note to Mrs. Brent and include the recipe in it? Then, we will offer it to anyone else who expresses an interest. That should quell all the rumours."

"Must I give it to that woman? She leaves a bad taste in my mouth," Aunt Bea protested.

Abby could scarcely hold back a giggle as she thought that some might describe her aunt's cake in such a fashion. But she brought herself to order. "I think it would be wise, Aunt Bea. After all, she is the only one to express an overt interest in it, and we must show everyone that we are not being secretive."

"Very well. As soon as I have finished breakfast, I'll write to her."

Lady Jeffrey's cooperation started Abby's day off well. And she still had her ride in the Park with Mr. Russell to look forward to, making it easier to ignore Phoebe's tragic face. After all, she was only doing her duty as her sister's guardian. At least she could put that problem from her mind during her time with Mr. Russell.

In spite of herself, Abby was pleased that he had invited her for a second drive after expressing his pleasure in their first one. Of course, she did not expect a marriage proposal from Mr. Russell, but his company made her stay in London more enjoyable.

"WE HAVE DELIGHTFUL WEATHER today," Mr. Russell began after they reached the Park. He was reluctant to broach the reason for his invitation.

"Yes, it is marvellous. Spring is such a delightful time."

"Yes." Having exhausted such an innocuous subject, Mr. Russell sought another. "Are you enjoying your Season?"

"It is certainly exciting," Abby said, unwilling to confess how overwhelmed she had been with all the unforeseen difficulties.

"Exciting?"

"We had a burglar," she confessed.

"When?"

"Last evening, while we were at the musicale."

Mr. Russell felt protective towards his companion, but he told himself it was only because she was living in his cousin's house. "Is everyone all right?"

"Oh, yes. I believe Mrs. Healy was frightened, but she is all right now."

"Was anything taken? Richard will need to know if..."

"No, nothing at all. Well, that is not true. It seems the burglar stole from the pantry."

"Ah. There is a great deal of poverty and hunger among the lower levels of society." Mr. Russell was intrigued by Abby's quivering lips. "You find that amusing?"

"No! Of course not. It is just...well, our burglar only took Aunt Bea's lemon cake." She had not intended to tell Mr. Russell anything about that, but she could not allow him to believe she was so hard-hearted.

"The lemon cake? That is all that was taken? How strange."

"You can see my amusement. I find it difficult to believe our burglar was truly hungry. He passed up a ham, several chickens and various vegetables. Even Monsieur Pierre's famous pastries were ignored."

"It would be ungentlemanly of me to comment on your burglar's taste," Mr. Russell said, grinning. "Have you no idea why he would be so interested in that particular item?"

Abby hesitated, but she decided to confide in Mr. Russell. After all, he would not believe such a ridiculous tale. "Unfortunately, I do. You see, some people believe... that is, it is rumoured that my aunt's cake has magical powers."

Mr. Russell stared at her in surprise until a shout drew his attention back to his horses.

"Her lemon cake is a fountain of youth, perhaps? Maybe I should have tried it."

"No. A love potion," Abby said quietly.

The involuntary jerk Mr. Russell gave to his reins had his horses protesting. "A love potion? You are teasing, are you not, Miss Milhouse?"

"I am only repeating what is being said. Of course, it is not true. There is no such thing as a love potion."

"No, of course not," Mr. Russell agreed, while he recalled Lady Jeffrey's strange behaviour of their first visit. "As I recall, my cousin partook of the lemon cake."

"He may have. But since it is a ridiculous assertion, Mr. Russell, it does not matter."

"True. Still, I will enjoy teasing him about it. Unless, of course, I am to keep this information a secret."

"No, not at all. In fact, my aunt is going to offer her recipe to some of the ladies of the ton. She had not before because it is an old family recipe, but she agreed to share it with others, since it is so popular."

Mr. Russell looked at his companion in admiration. Whatever had transpired to bring about such a rumour, Miss Milhouse had come up with an effective antidote. And one was needed. A rumour like that could destroy their social standing. Using trickery to gain a husband was not unheard of, but one should never be caught.

"That is most generous of your aunt, but I can assure you I will not rob her of her treasure," Mr. Russell responded with a laugh.

"I did not think you would, sir, just on the remote possibility that the rumour had any value. After all, you are not seeking a mate," Abby said drily.

"Speaking of marriage," Mr. Russell began, deciding he would receive no better opportunity to introduce the main reason for their ride, "many families would be delighted to receive the offer Lord Norfolk made."

"How did you . . ." Abby began, surprised.

"Lord Norfolk came to me after his interview with you. He was most disturbed by your denial of his request and asked that I plead with you." Reading Abby's rejection of his interference in her eyes, Mr. Russell hastily added, "I am, after all, a close friend of Lord Norfolk and will quite willingly vouch for his character."

"It is not his character, sir, but his age and his experience that I question."

"But it is that experience that puts his character to question in your mind, is it not?"

Abby's cheeks flushed and she stared straight ahead.

"You are basing your decision on the same rumour mill that pronounces your aunt's cake to be a love potion."

That telling remark disturbed Abby. But she refused to budge from the position she had taken. "Are you telling me that Lord Norfolk has not . . ." she hesitated, unable to delicately ask such a question.

Mr. Russell was almost as embarrassed as his companion. Discussing this subject with an unmarried woman was not acceptable. "Lord Norfolk said it was impossible to explain to you about . . . I understand his frustration."

"Mr. Russell, if you had a daughter, would you want Lord Norfolk as her husband?"

Her question took him aback, and he carefully considered before answering. "I understand your point. Phoebe is young and innocent. But I know Lord Norfolk to be an honourable man who would never betray your sister's trust." Abby opened her mouth but Mr. Russell continued. "Also, Miss Milhouse, while Miss Phoebe is stunningly beautiful, she is not…she will be content with much less than Miss Mary, or even Miss Kitty. She wants protection from the harshness of life, balls, pretty gowns, a loving husband. A young man is too demanding for Miss Phoebe. He would expect too much from her."

His last point made an impression on Abby. For the first time, she truly considered her sister's suitor. She had rejected him out of hand because of his age and experience. But if what Mr. Russell said was true, and she thought he had accurately read Phoebe's mind, a man like Lord Norfolk was exactly what Phoebe would need in a husband.

"Lord Norfolk has a good friend in you, Mr. Russell," she said quietly.

"You mean you will accept his suit?"

"No. But I will reconsider my decision."

"I am pleased, Miss Milhouse. May I tell Lord Norfolk what you have said?"

"Yes, please." Though he gave her a warm smile, Abby did not return it. With their conversation drawing to a natural close, Abby realized Mr. Russell had not invited her to drive with him because he enjoyed her companionship, but because he had promised Lord Norfolk he would plead his case. It was a dismaying conclusion.

"What of your other sisters?" Mr. Russell asked.

"They are quite well. Would you object to our returning home now, Mr. Russell? I am afraid I have developed the headache. Perhaps it is all this deep thought that has caused it," she joked feebly, wanting to cry but refusing to ask herself why.

"Of course not, Miss Milhouse. I hope I have not caused you any distress. But truly, Lord Norfolk is—"

"Please, Mr. Russell, you have persuaded me to reconsider. You need not continue to praise Lord Norfolk."

Her rather abrupt interruption surprised Mr. Russell, but he attributed it to her headache. As quickly as possible, he turned his horses in the direction of the nearest gate to the Park. "We will have you home in no time. Perhaps a cup of tea and a rest will relieve you of the pain. Will you be attending Lady Westerly's ball this evening?"

"Yes. You may tell Lord Norfolk he may dance with Phoebe, and...and take her for a drive in the Park tomorrow, if he pleases. But ask him to wait a few days before coming to talk to me again."

"You are most generous, Miss Milhouse. Please believe I would not plead his cause were I not convinced it is for the best."

Abby sank her teeth into her bottom lip. The imaginary headache was fast becoming a reality. She said nothing, and Mr. Russell, seeing how pale his companion was, hurried his horses along the crowded street.

AFTER LEAVING Miss Milhouse, Mr Russell continued on to Lord Norfolk's. He was admitted at once, and found Lord Norfolk at the door of his library, eagerly grasping his arm. "Come in, Giles, come in. Did you talk to her? What did she say?"

"I talked to her, Jason, and assured her you would never betray Miss Phoebe's love. I also assured her you had a sterling character in spite of your many romantic assignations."

"Giles, you did not!"

Mr. Russell laughed at the man's horrified expression. "Well, I did assure her of your good character...but I did not confirm the rumours circulating about you."

"Ah. And her response?"

"She agreed to reconsider her decision."

With a loud whoop, Lord Norfolk grabbed his friend and danced him about the room.

"Here now, Norfolk, enough of that. Besides, you are not yet accepted."

"But I am not forbidden to see her, am I?"

"No. Miss Milhouse said you may dance with Miss Phoebe this evening at Lady Westerly's ball, and you may take her for a ride in the Park tomorrow, if you wish. But she asked that you wait a few days before approaching her again to request her sister's hand in marriage."

"Giles, you are a genius! I had not hoped for half as much. I was preparing to elope if Phoebe would agree to it. I can never thank you enough, my friend. Whatever I can do for you, you have only to ask."

"I'll try to think of something," Mr. Russell assured him.

"I know you had to give up precious work time to visit with Miss Milhouse. If you would like some assistance or..."

"No, no, Norfolk. It was not such an onerous task. I find Miss Milhouse a charming companion. And you must admit she is intelligent and open-minded."

"I will agree to anything you say, Russell. Shall I see you this evening at Lady Westerly's?"

"Yes, I believe I'll put in an appearance. For a few moments, that is."

"You are becoming quite the social butterfly," Lord Norfolk teased, his grin stretching across his entire face.

Mr. Russell said nothing. His friend had little awareness of him at the moment. All his thoughts were focussed on the object of his love.

Taking his leave, Mr. Russell returned home to put in an hour or two of work before dining with his cousin. And then he, too, would prepare for his social outing. He was looking forward to it, though, of course, it was only because he felt in the mood for company.

CHAPTER THIRTEEN

"YOU HAVE NOT SAID how your visit with Miss Milhouse about Lord Norfolk's offer progressed. Was she upset?" Lord Harrington asked as he and his cousin strolled the short distance to Lady Westerly's ball.

"No," Mr. Russell said with a reminiscent smile. "She is a most remarkable young woman. I assured her of Lord Norfolk's good character and then explained why I thought the marriage would succeed. She listened to my arguments and agreed to reconsider her decision."

"I am impressed. If I should ever need assistance in matters of the heart, I shall call upon you."

"Rather, you should hope for the cooperation of as intelligent a woman as Miss Milhouse."

"Perhaps Miss Milhouse is that elusive woman to coax you back into our world."

Mr. Russell made no comment, only smiling as he strolled along. He had already realized Miss Milhouse was an unusual young lady. She was the antithesis of his first wife, a giddy young girl with no thoughts in her head. The question was not Miss Milhouse's suitability, but his willingness to be caught.

"It would certainly provide Thomas with a family. He and young Jonathan seem most compatible."

"If he were any more so, I would think I had adopted the boy," Mr. Russell said drily.

"Well, you would if you married Miss Milhouse."

"I am not yet at the altar, cousin. Besides, *you* are the one in search of a bride. Have you found anyone to appeal to you yet?"

"There are many beauties being offered this Season."

"What has that to say to anything?"

Lord Harrington shrugged his shoulders. He was not prepared to examine his own feelings, much less discuss them with his cousin.

Their arrival at Lady Westerly's precluded any further questioning, and both men eagerly mounted the steps to the mansion. After greeting their hostess and her blushing daughter, the two surveyed the ballroom.

Without awareness of how closely attuned their minds were, Lord Harrington asked, "I do not see them. Do you?"

"No, I—there, by the column with the pink garlands." Both men moved as one in that direction, though there was no unseemly haste in their manner.

Lord Norfolk had been one of the early arrivals at the ball, an unusual occurrence for him, and had immediately sought out the Milhouse ladies. Abby had decided not to inform Phoebe of the treat in store for her, afraid her excitement would overwhelm her. It would not be the first time her emotions had given her a fever.

When Lord Norfolk approached them, Phoebe frantically signalled him with her eyes, but she only received a blissful smile in return. The smitten man first approached Abby, taking her hand and raising it to his lips. "Thank you, Miss Milhouse. I shall await your pleasure."

"Thank you for your patience, Lord Norfolk." She looked at her sister, who was staring at them goggle-eyed, and called her to her side. "Phoebe, I believe Lord Norfolk would enjoy dancing with you. Do you have any dances left?"

A beatific smile broke onto her sister's face and Abby thought she had never looked more beautiful. Lord Norfolk agreed. "Oh, yes, thank you, Abby! Yes, I have several left," Phoebe assured her suitor with a sidelong look at Abby to see if she would quibble at more than one dance with her beloved.

Mary and Kitty watched in surprise as Lord Norfolk signed their sister's card and then signed each of their cards once. However, when he asked for Abby's card, she denied it.

"I appreciate your offer, my lord, but I would prefer that we sit and talk rather than dance. I hope to have a closer acquaintance with you."

"That would be my pleasure, Miss Milhouse."

"And I would not object if Phoebe wished to join us, should she be free."

Since Lord Norfolk could only have the two dances for which he had signed with Miss Phoebe, he was appreciative of additional time. "It would be my pleasure, Miss Milhouse," he said again.

After Lord Norfolk departed to greet acquaintances, promising Phoebe to return as soon as possible, the sisters gathered around Abby.

"You have changed your mind?" Phoebe demanded ecstatically.

"No, not yet. But I have agreed to reconsider my decision." She smiled at her second sister. "I only ever wanted your happiness, Phoebe."

"I know, Abby, but truly, I love Lord Norfolk."

"Ssh, love, I understand. We will see. You must dance with others, however. There are several gentlemen approaching."

Phoebe and Kitty turned and greeted the men, but Mary squeezed Abby's hand. "I think you have done the right thing, Abby."

"What has she done?" Lady Jeffrey asked as she returned from visiting with friends.

"I have agreed to reconsider Lord Norfolk's offer."

"Wonderful! I am glad you did, because I'm not sure we will be able to count on my lemon cake any more. Several of the ladies asked about it, and I did as you asked."

"You offered the recipe?"

"Yes. I told them to call on the morrow and I would give it to them."

Abby groaned silently. She would not look forward to their arrival in the morning. One of the gentlemen approached Mary and Abby for a dance after signing Phoebe and Kitty's cards. Mary graciously assented, but Abby smilingly refused. "Thank you, Mr. Bradford, but I do not dance this evening."

"It is my loss, Miss Milhouse," the gentleman said with a bow before walking away.

"What do you mean, you are not dancing?" Lady Jeffrey demanded.

"Why did you say that?" Mary asked simultaneously.

"I do not care to dance this evening," Abby said coolly. "It is time I paid more attention to my duties as a chaperon."

Both ladies protested, Lady Jeffrey saying, "I am here to act as chaperon. You should be dancing, my girl. As I said, my lemon cake will not—"

"Good evening, ladies," Lord Harrington said, Mr. Russell echoing his greeting.

Mary greeted Lord Harrington eagerly and Lady Jeffrey smiled. Abby nodded to both men and then turned her attention to an elderly lady standing nearby. "Good evening, Mrs. Rutledge. Are you enjoying the Season?"

Abby's family and the two gentlemen stared at her. Lady Jeffrey finally broke the silence. "If you are looking for dancing partners, gentlemen, I would offer but I fear I could not last through a dance without expiring. Perhaps you should ask Mary."

Lord Harrington followed her directions at once, though he gave Mary a speaking glance. When she looked at her card and discovered he had signed it in two places, her heart fluttered. Mr. Russell stared after Miss Milhouse, a frown on his face. He turned to discover Lady Jeffrey studying him.

"What has occurred to disturb Miss Milhouse?" he asked quietly.

"I do not know. She changed her mind about Lord Norfolk, but I do not see how that would have affected her so. But she has refused to dance with anyone this evening."

It relieved Mr. Russell that he was not the first to be rejected by Miss Milhouse, but his disappointment was disturbing. He had not expected it to matter so much to him. He was also puzzled. What could have occurred from the time he left her until this evening that would have disturbed her so?

Lord Harrington turned back to Mary after absentmindedly signing the other young ladies' cards. He whispered, "Is Miss Milhouse unhappy with my cousin?"

"I did not think so, but she has acted strangely several times this evening," Mary whispered in return, her eyes on her sister.

"Did Miss Milhouse and Miss Phoebe—"

"Good evening, Miss Mary," Mr. Morrison said, surprising the other two.

"Oh, good evening, Mr. Morrison," Mary said politely while wishing the man anywhere but beside her. "You are acquainted with Lord Harrington?"

Mr. Morrison stiffly acknowledged the other man before saying, "I called on you today hoping to take you for a drive, but you were not at home." His accusing tones jarred Mary.

"I'm sorry. I would have enjoyed it, but I was otherwise engaged."

With me! Lord Harrington thought triumphantly, a scowl on his face. He wished Mary would send the man on his way.

"Perhaps I could escort you tomorrow," Mr. Morrison said more hopefully.

"That would be—" Mary began before being interrupted.

"She will be unable to accompany you tomorrow. We have already made plans."

That Mr. Morrison was affronted was clear to both members of his audience. He directed a questioning look down his long nose at Mary, who, after a glance at Lord Harrington, murmured, "I'm so sorry."

Mr. Morrison's abrupt departure evoked a soft, "Oh, dear," from Mary.

"Why do you bother with that bore?" Lord Harrington demanded more harshly than he intended. "Are you not interested in your sister's happiness?"

"Yes, I am," Mary said coolly, disturbed by his highhandedness, "but I am also concerned with my own."

"You think to find happiness with *him*?" Lord Harrington asked incredulously.

"I am no beauty, my lord, like Phoebe, but I hope some day to have children of my own. For that, a husband is required. So far, Mr. Morrison is the only one to show an interest," Mary said coldly, angry with herself and the man she loved. "Excuse me. I must speak with my sister."

LORD HARRINGTON found his cousin leaning against a wall of the ballroom. "You look like Byron, scowling across the room."

Mr. Russell pushed himself upright. "Perhaps I should go home."

"Here now, Giles, do you give up so easily?" Richard demanded, alarmed at the despair voiced by his cousin.

"There is nothing to give up. I simply find this distasteful. Do you join me?"

"You cannot go, Giles. Have you forgotten you signed the dance cards of the younger Milhouse ladies?"

"Damn!" Mr. Russell said under his breath.

"Perhaps you can engage Miss Milhouse in conversation if she is not dancing. That way you will not be interrupted by every jackanapes who has signed her card."

Mr. Russell brightened up at his cousin's observations. "You are right, Richard. I should have thought of that."

ABBY WISHED TO GO HOME and hide. She felt like crying after refusing Mr. Russell's invitation to dance. But she was obliged to stay for the sake of her sisters. After all, it was her failure as a chaperon that had caused all the difficulties. She should have understood more than anyone, much less Mr. Russell, that Phoebe needed an older, less demanding husband. But she had been too concerned about her own feelings, convinced by her aunt that she was a blushing debutante.

"Miss Milhouse, it is so generous of your aunt to share her recipe with the rest of us," Mrs. Brent said, appearing at Abby's side. "Are all four of you spoken for and no longer have need of its powers?"

"What powers?" Abby asked sweetly when she would have preferred to pull the woman's hair out.

"Oh, come now, Miss Milhouse. You know what is being said."

With a cool smile, Abby said, "I never listen to gossip, Mrs. Brent. Excuse me, my aunt is calling me." Lady Jeffrey would have been surprised, had she heard her niece's remark.

THE EVENING PROGRESSED with varying degrees of success. Lady Jeffrey enjoyed great popularity as Mamas of unmarried daughters were eager to learn the secret of her lemon cake. Though she willingly agreed to share the recipe with any who asked, she refused to deny the reports of its special powers. By the end of the evening, the rumours concerning the lemon cake were gargantuan.

Phoebe found the evening most enjoyable. Reunited with her love, she floated about the room in a haze of happiness. The young men fortunate enough to dance with the toast of the Season found renewed determination to press their suits because of her beauty.

Not all the gentlemen were entranced with Miss Phoebe, however. Lord Abbott arrived late at the ball, escorting a very attractive young lady. Kitty, who always kept watch for his arrival, was stunned. Never had he offered to escort her to a social event. Such a slight enraged her, and the feverish glitter in her eyes drew many men.

Abby, from her vantage point among the chaperons, observed Peter's entrance and wished he were as easy to guide now as he had been as a child. Or even several months ago when Kitty had led him around by the nose. With a sinking heart, Abby wondered if she had made another mistake in not allowing Kitty to become engaged prior to their departure for London. Depression seized her, but she remained seated, determined to do her duty as chaperon.

When Kitty was returned to Abby's side, she squeezed her sister's hand in sympathy. The younger girl smiled tremulously at her sister and raised her chin. Abby whispered, "You have always been a fighter, my love. Don't give up now."

Before Kitty could answer, they were interrupted by Lord Abbott and his companion. "Good evening, ladies. I believe you are acquainted with Miss Pilling, are you not?"

"Of course we are, Lord Abbott. You appear to great advantage this evening, Miss Pilling," Abby said as she nudged her sister to acknowledge the pair.

"Yes, you do. In fact, the two of you make a handsome couple," Kitty enthused bitterly. "Shall we be hearing an announcement soon?"

The panic on Peter's face would have been humorous had it not been for Miss Pilling's blushing cheeks.

Abby rushed in. "You must excuse Kitty, Miss Pilling. She has weddings on the brain because we will shortly be announcing her sister's engagement."

"Phoebe?" Peter asked abruptly. "I don't suppose it is Willie?"

"No, it is not, Peter."

"Oh, lord, I'd best find him. He will be brokenhearted."

"That is normal for a London Season, is it not? Those who love are betrayed by cold, unfeeling—"

"Kitty! Aunt Bea is calling to you," Abby insisted, interrupting her sister's tirade. Lord Peter, white-faced, watched her sister stalk away, while Miss Pilling looked at Abby in confusion.

"Is Miss Kitty Milhouse upset?" she asked timidly, an understatement that led Abby to the verge of hysteria.

"A headache only, my dear. Pay no mind to her. Once the pain starts, she has no idea what she is saying."

Peter, who knew Kitty never had headaches, was scorching Abby with his eyes. She began a conversation with Miss Pilling about the latest fashion while she watched Kitty sit down beside her aunt. She hoped Aunt Bea could restore her sister's equanimity.

"Good evening, Lord Abbott, Miss Pilling. Hello again, Miss Milhouse. Are you enjoying the evening?" Mr. Russell asked genially while he carefully watched Abby's face. He was at least gratified not to find rejection there.

In truth, Abby was delighted by his arrival. She had no more platitudes to offer Miss Pilling, and neither the young lady nor her companion were eager conversationalists.

Mr. Russell chatted a few moments but forestalled Abby's attempt to withdraw. "Would you excuse the two of us? There is someone I would like Miss Milhouse to meet." He strolled away with her on his arm without a backward glance.

"Who is it that I am to meet, sir?" Abby asked coolly.

"No one. I had simply run out of meaningless chatter and thought perhaps you had, also."

"Thank you for your rescue, then, Mr. Russell. I will return to my aunt now."

"I accept that you are not dancing, Miss Milhouse, but have you foresworn punch also?"

"Of course not, but—"

"Good." With a wave of his hand, he caught the attention of a waiter and gave him directions to deliver two glasses of punch to the chairs to which he was now leading her.

"Did your sister react as jubilantly to your change of mind as did Lord Norfolk?" he asked pleasantly once they were seated.

"I do not know Lord Norfolk's reaction, but Phoebe was happy."

"Norfolk danced me round the room before I could say nay!" Mr. Russell said in disgruntled amusement. "'Happy' seems a rather tame description in comparison."

Abby could not hold back a smile as she pictured the scene. "And I'm sure you made a lovely couple," she said silkily.

"You naughty girl, to tease me when I only sought your sister's happiness."

"Girl hardly seems an appropriate appellation, sir, for a woman beyond the age of giddiness," Abby pointed out.

Mr. Russell smiled at the beautiful young woman beside him. "Anyone who looks as much like an angel as you," he said, impulsively touching a white-gold curl, "might not be described as naughty, but most certainly is too young to consider herself on the shelf."

Abby clamped down on her response to his compliment. There was no future here, and she must not be misled by pleasant conversation. "Mary and Lord Harrington have taken to the floor. He is an excellent dancer."

"I would be pleased to demonstrate my own expertise if you would only accompany me."

Abby flashed him a glance before lowering her lids. "Thank you, but I must resume my duties as chaperon. If you will excuse me?"

Mr. Russell rose with her and remained by her side until she joined Lady Jeffrey, but no more words were spoken between them.

MARY WAS HORRIFIED both with her behaviour and that of Lord Harrington. She considered seeking out Mr. Morrison and apologizing, but she was too embarrassed. When Lord Harrington arrived for their first dance, she greeted him coolly.

Though her look warned him, Lord Harrington could not resist saying, "Would you prefer to sit out this dance, Mary?"

"No, my lord. I would like to dance."

Since it was a country dance, conversation was limited, but Lord Harrington did his best.

"I did not appear too high-handed earlier?" he asked with a smile intended to charm.

Mary only gave him a wide-eyed stare before they were separated by the dance. When they came together again, Lord Harrington tried once more. "You will come out with me tomorrow, will you not? We must determine why your sister and my cousin are at odds."

Mary hesitated as she hid her disappointment that his only reason for asking her out was his cousin's happiness, but she nodded.

He could not engage her in more conversation during the dance, but he contented himself with the thought that he had another dance with her that evening and a ride in the Park on the morrow.

Lord Harrington was wrong, however. The Milhouse party left midway through the evening. And after a private discussion with Abby and Aunt Bea, Mary, unbeknownst to Lord Harrington until her note arrived the next morning, cancelled their scheduled ride in the Park.

CHAPTER FOURTEEN

"WHAT SHOULD I DO?" Mary asked painfully. She and her eldest sister and Lady Jeffrey were gathered in her bedroom after their early departure from the ball.

"Do you think Lord Harrington is interested?" Lady Jeffrey asked eagerly. "After all, he did eat my lemon cake."

"No," Mary said bluntly, offering nothing more.

"But why would he continue to extend invitations if he has no interest in you?"

Mary ducked her head, not anxious to reveal her part in their harmless conspiracy.

Abby and Aunt Bea exchanged worried looks, various scandals flitting through her minds. "Well?" prompted Lady Jeffrey.

"Lord Harrington had decided Abby would make a good wife for his cousin." She ignored Abby's gasp and continued. "I thought it was a wonderful idea, so I agreed to help him. He kept asking me out to discover Abby's feelings and I . . . agreed because I enjoyed his company." She hung her head in embarrassment.

"Lord Harrington would be better advised to determine his cousin's feelings," Abby said crisply. "Then he would know to look elsewhere for a wife for Mr. Russell."

Abby's controlled tones drew sympathetic glances from the other two. Aunt Bea said briskly, "Do you find Mr. Morrison acceptable, Mary?"

The young lady bit her lip and looked away, saying, "He is the only one to show an interest."

"Mary, you do not have to marry," Abby urged. "We can remain spinsters together."

"I know, Abby," Mary said with a sweet smile. "But I truly do want a family. And Mr. Morrison is a kind man."

"Very well," Aunt Bea intervened. "Then you should write two notes, my love, one to Mr. Morrison stating you have cancelled your ride with Lord Harrington, should he still be willing to drive you, and one to Lord Harrington telling him you are unable to accompany him."

"Yes," Mary agreed in mournful tones. She knew it was best, but she would miss the hours spent in Lord Harrington's company. Afraid her determination would weaken, Mary wrote her notes before going to bed and gave them to Rose to be delivered first thing in the morning. Then she cried herself to sleep.

"I HAVE DECIDED you were right, Abby," Kitty said abruptly the next morning at the breakfast table.

Surprised, Abby asked cautiously, "About what?"

"About Peter. He obviously cares nothing for me. I must look elsewhere for a husband."

"Are you sure, Kitty? I believe Peter still cares for you."

"I do not. Not once since his arrival has he shown any partiality for me."

"That is not true, Kitty," Mary said. "From his first visit, you were cold to him, scarcely speaking to him and flirting with any gentleman but him."

"I may have done so," Kitty said stoutly, "but only with good reason."

"And what reason was that?" Abby asked softly.

"Because I was afraid he had already forgotten me, and I wanted him to—to show he still wanted me." To everyone's amazement, Kitty burst into tears, burying her face in her hands.

"Oh, my poor dear," Abby said as she moved to take her sister into her arms.

Lady Jeffrey shook her head. "Who'd have thought it?" she said. "I believed that child was indifferent to the boy."

"I think he thought so, too," Mary said quietly as Abby led the weeping Kitty from the room. "Excuse me, Aunt Bea. I will just go and offer my assistance to Abby."

Shortly afterward, while Lady Jeffrey was still nursing her second cup of tea, Abby returned to the table.

"Is Kitty all right?"

"Yes, Aunt Bea. But I feel her terrible unhappiness is my fault."

"Why?"

"I did not believe Kitty really loved Peter. If I had understood her better, she would now be engaged to him. I seem to have made a mess of everything."

"How can you say that, Abby dear? After all, Phoebe is making a most advantageous marriage and is ecstatically happy."

"Had it been left to me, she would still be miserable. It took a stranger to point out my own sister's needs."

"You are being too hard on yourself, child. You have done your best."

"But I wanted them to be happy, and instead I have made them miserable," Abby protested sorrowfully.

"Well, Phoebe is now happy, and we will see what we can do about Lord Abbott. Perhaps we can ask him to call and serve him my lemon cake."

"I suspect the eligible young men of London will swiftly tire of your lemon cake, since it may be served in every drawing-room in the city. Unless you convinced them it has no special powers?" Abby's suggestion was a question, but her aunt refused to meet her eye.

"I gave out my recipe as you asked," the old lady said defensively, refusing to admit she had increased the rumours, if anything, by her refusal to deny them.

"Oh, dear."

MR. RUSSELL was in an irritable mood, a fact noted at once by everyone from his valet down to the youngest footman. Normally an even-tempered man, he was irked by everything this morning. "This steak is not cooked to my liking," he snapped at his butler, a long-time retainer.

Bates responded with a guarded look at his master. "I shall return it to the chef at once, Sir."

"No, no, it will be fine." Mr. Russell felt ashamed of his bad mood. "I'm sorry, Bates. I'm in poor frame this morning."

It was such consideration and honesty that endeared Mr. Russell to his servants. "Perhaps you would enjoy a special pastry?" Bates offered, showing his master the vol-au-vents filled with cream.

"Papa!" Thomas's call forestalled his response as Mr. Russell's son rushed through the door, followed more slowly by a shy Jonathan.

"Good morning, Thomas. Does Mr. Brownlee teach you to announce your arrival in such a fashion?" Mr. Russell asked testily.

The two boys exchanged a look before Thomas said, "Sorry, Papa. Mr. Brownlee is ill today and cannot teach us. I told him to return to his bed as he was very flushed and had a headache. I knew you would want that," the boy said self-righteously.

Mr. Russell groaned inwardly at the thought of having the care of two active boys for the day. "Sit down and enjoy our chef's pastries while I determine what to do with you."

Bates served the two boys willingly. Thomas was spoiled by the staff, but his father ensured good behaviour. And Jonathan, who had become Thomas's shadow, had been adopted by the household. However, Bates realized his master was not in the mood to deal with the two fugitives from the schoolroom.

"Sir, Mr. Wilson is visiting Riverview today, and will return tomorrow. Perhaps the two young gentlemen would enjoy an overnight stay in the country."

Though the butler was speaking to the man, the boys' eyes grew large in eager anticipation of his answer.

"An admirable solution, Bates, if you think these two would not interfere too much with his duties." Mr. Wilson was in charge of overseeing Mr. Russell's various estates, including Riverview, located close to London.

"We wouldn't, Papa, I promise," Thomas assured him while Jonathan nodded.

"I believe Mr. Wilson would enjoy their company, Sir," Bates said, winking at the boys.

"Would your sister approve of your accompanying my man of business on such a trip, Jonathan?" Mr. Russell asked.

"I think—I hope so, sir."

"Very well. Eat your pastries and I will write a note to Miss Milhouse."

The boys exchanged excited looks before attacking their second breakfast.

Mr. Russell retired to the library, pleased to have a reason to approach Miss Milhouse. He was still puzzled by her withdrawal last evening.

Before the note could be completed, Bates interrupted him. "Pardon me, Sir, but a Lord Abbott has called and desires a private interview with you. He says it is urgent."

Frowning, Mr. Russell could think of no reason Lord Abbott would call, particularly on an 'urgent' matter. "You'd better show him in, Bates, and," he added as he signed his name to the note, "have this taken to Miss Milhouse at once."

Mr. Russell rose to greet the pale young man who entered. Once they were both seated, he waited for his caller to speak.

"Last night, I overheard Lord Norfolk tell someone that Miss Milhouse has agreed to entertain his offer for Phoebe because you interceded for him," Lord Peter said abruptly.

A dark eyebrow raised above one green eye, but Mr. Russell said nothing.

"Sir, I know you have no reason to help me, but I am desperate." Lord Abbott's face reflected both his youth and his pain.

"I assume your interest is with Miss Kitty?" A jerky nod was the young man's only response. "But I thought you and Miss Kitty had a long-standing, er, agreement."

Lord Abbott sprang from his chair to pace the room. "I thought so, too. We would have been engaged if her sister had agreed. But since I've come to Town, nothing has gone right. She is always surrounded by other men, and she is cold and disagreeable whenever I approach her."

"Pardon me, but were you not escorting Miss Pilling last evening?" Mr. Russell asked casually.

With flushed cheeks, Lord Abbott muttered, "That was Willie's idea. He thought I should make Kitty jealous. But she implied I would be making an offer for Miss Pilling, and I could barely escape from the young lady without doing so. As it was, I felt a cad.''

"I can imagine.''

"So I decided to ask for your help. Would you talk to Abby—I mean Miss Milhouse—for me? Tell her I am sure it is Kitty I love? Would you do that for me? My parents have no objection to the match. It is only Miss Milhouse who has refused to agree.''

Mr. Russell grinned at the idea of approaching Abby a second time to bring about another of her sisters' marriage.

Lord Abbott, his eyes anxiously watching the older man, saw the smile and said eagerly, "You will help me?''

Holding up his hands in protest, Mr. Russell said, "Please, Lord Abbott, I am no miracle-worker.'' He watched the young man's face fall before adding, "But I will talk to Miss Milhouse on your behalf.''

"Oh, thank you, Mr. Russell! I will do anything in return for your assistance!''

Mr. Russell smiled ruefully. He was certainly storing up a lot of gratitude of late. "That is kind of you, Lord Abbott. But please remember, I am only going to speak to Miss Milhouse. I suspect Miss Kitty will be the determining factor.''

"I know but . . . I can bear this no longer. Please tell her I love Kitty now more than ever.''

"I will do my best,'' Mr. Russell promised, rising and coming round the desk to pat Lord Abbott on the back.

"When?''

"I shall drive over and offer to escort Miss Milhouse to the Park today.''

"Shall I wait here?''

With a rueful shake of his head, Mr. Russell pictured Bates's reaction to keeping an eye on his nervous guest for several hours. "Why do you not go back to Sir William's, and I will send you word when I return."

MR. RUSSELL FOLLOWED his travelling coach to the Milhouse residence. Miss Milhouse had returned an answer to his note, giving her permission and promising to have a bag packed for Jonathan. He felt sure she would be at home, waiting to see her brother off.

Mr. Russell and the two boys were shown into the parlour where Abby and Aunt Bea were waiting, along with Mr. Morrison.

"Good morning, Mr. Russell, Thomas," Abby said as she extended a hand to Jonathan as he rushed to her side. "Are you acquainted with Mr. Morrison?"

The two men exchanged greetings, Mr. Russell wondering if the man had a tendre for Miss Milhouse. His question was answered almost immediately when Mary entered the room.

"I am ready now, Mr. Morrison," Mary said, before realizing other guests had arrived. "Oh, Mr. Russell, forgive me. I did not see you."

"Not at all, Miss Mary. May I say you look delightful this morning," Mr. Russell said, all the while wondering where the couple was going. He was sure his cousin had told him last evening he was taking Miss Mary for a carriage ride today.

"Thank you, sir. If you will excuse us, Mr. Morrison is taking me for a ride in the Park."

After they had departed, Abby said, "Are you sure your man of business does not mind being burdened with another charge?"

"Of course he does not."

"Mr. Wilson is a great gun, Miss Milhouse," Thomas added. "He says there are some new puppies at the estate."

"Ah, that makes a visit imperative, does it not?" Abby said with a warm smile at the boy.

How well she understands young boys, Mr. Russell thought as his son drew closer to the young woman, anxious to tell her all about the puppies.

When the boys and Mr. Wilson had been sent on their way with promises of good behaviour, Mr. Russell invited Miss Milhouse to join him in the parade in the Park. "It is a lovely day," he added as inducement.

"Yes, it is, Mr. Russell, but I'm afraid I cannot."

Whatever had disturbed Miss Milhouse the evening before was still affecting her, Mr. Russell decided. "I have something important to discuss with you, Miss Milhouse," he said, glancing over at Lady Jeffrey.

"I do not see what..." Abby began, but the seriousness of Mr. Russell's look found her changing her mind.

"Thank you, Mr. Russell, I will just fetch a wrap and my bonnet."

When the parlour door closed behind her, Lady Jeffrey looked up from her needle-point. "You will not upset my niece, will you, Mr. Russell?"

Startled, he stared at the lady. "I hope not, Lady Jeffrey. Did I upset her yesterday?"

"She felt she should have realized Lord Norfolk was perfect for Phoebe. It made her feel she had failed in her duty as guardian to her sister."

"I never intended to even suggest such a thing!" Mr. Russell exclaimed.

"I felt sure you did not, sir, but Abby is very sensitive."

"Yes," Mr. Russell said with a frown, his mind on the young lady.

"Would you care for a piece of my lemon cake, Mr. Russell?" Lady Jeffrey asked genially.

"No, thank you, ma'am," Mr. Russell said absent-mindedly.

Before Lady Jeffrey could try to persuade him to sample her particular delicacy, Abby returned. She had spent as much time wondering what Mr. Russell could want to say to her as she had preparing for their outing.

ONCE THEY HAD ASCENDED into Mr. Russell's high-perch phaeton, he murmured, "May I dismiss my tiger?"

Abby hesitated, but then nodded briefly.

"Wait here, Jimmy. We will return in an hour."

The pair remained silent until they reached Hyde Park, Mr. Russell relaxed, concentrating on his horses, and Miss Milhouse tensed, imagining greater and greater catastrophes.

When Mr. Russell finally addressed her, she almost fell from her precarious seat. He clasped her arm in concern.

"Are you all right, Miss Milhouse?"

"Yes, of course. Please, tell me why you asked me to accompany you."

"Miss Milhouse, it is nothing to alarm you. And it seems I owe you an apology. Your aunt says I offended you yesterday."

"Offended me?" Abby asked, distracted from her worries.

"Well, that is, she said I made you feel that you had not done your duty as guardian."

"Aunt Bea should not have burdened you with family difficulties."

"But Miss Milhouse, it is because you love your sister that you could not see clearly. And, most importantly, you listened to reason and did what was best for her."

Tears gathered in Abby's eyes and she blinked rapidly. "You are generous, sir, but I should have realized—"

"You have handled a difficult task well, my dear...Miss Milhouse," he added hurriedly at her surprised stare.

"Thank you." She composed herself and relaxed, suddenly aware of their surroundings. "My, I hope we have not caused any talk. I did not even realize we had joined the parade."

Mr. Russell grimaced. "I wish it were not so crowded," he said as he acknowledged the wave of a determined Mama. "I still have something of import to discuss with you."

Having almost forgotten that, Abby frowned. "What is it, Mr. Russell?"

"I hate to bring up the topic after my last effort disturbed you so."

"What are you talking about?" Abby asked in confusion.

"You would not dance with me last evening. In fact, you scarcely spoke to me."

"I do not understand, Mr. Russell," Abby protested, her cheeks red.

"I'm afraid I have come to plead for the hand of another of your sisters." Mr. Russell glanced over at his companion with an apologetic smile, to discover Miss Milhouse staring straight ahead, her cheeks white as a ghost's."

"Miss Milhouse, are you all right? I did not mean to startle you so!"

"I—I am fine, Mr. Russell," Abby whispered. Now that her heart had begun beating again, she forced herself to say, "In which of my sisters are you interested?"

It was Mr. Russell's turn to be surprised. "I? Oh, no, you misunderstand me, Miss Milhouse. I am speaking on another's behalf, just as I did for Lord Norfolk."

Relief flooded Abby, but she refused to acknowledge it. Her mind immediately jumped to the conclusion that he must be speaking for his cousin. Would Mary have her secret dream come true? Abby waited anxiously for Mr. Russell to continue.

"It may seem odd, but I am here to ask you to consider Lord Abbott's suit. He is desirous of marrying Miss Kitty, but he is afraid you continue to think him too young. And he is not sure Miss Kitty still cares for him."

Abby released a pent-up breath. Perhaps there would be happiness for two of her sisters, at least.

She was silent for so long, Mr. Russell added, "He truly seems to care for your sister, Miss Milhouse."

"Yes, I know he does."

"Does Miss Kitty...is she still interested in him?"

"Yes, Mr. Russell. You may tell Peter to come see me. I will be happy to accept his suit."

"I am sure he will appear on your doorstep as soon as possible. He is a most anxious suitor."

Abby only smiled. It was as well she had realized yesterday that Mr. Russell had only asked her to drive with him because of Lord Norfolk. Today it was because of dear Peter. As they returned to her residence, she smiled ruefully up at her companion. "I must remind you that I will only have one eligible sister after Peter calls, Mr. Russell. But should you arrive tomorrow with another suitor, I will entertain your suggestion."

Mr. Russell laughed and then raised her hand to his lips. "If I must find another suitor to entice you to drive with me, I shall do my best, Miss Milhouse."

"I shall look forward to your best, Mr. Russell." Abby smiled at him before entering the house, but there was a sadness in her eyes that Mr. Russell could not understand.

CHAPTER FIFTEEN

"BUT, PETER, you should have come to me, not Mr. Russell."

The young man hung his head as he muttered, "I know, Abby, but I was afraid you would say I was too young. But I swear to you, I love Kitty with all my heart."

"I believe you, Peter," Abby assured him. "Shall I call Kitty down so you may tell her?"

With a gulp, Peter pleaded, "Do not leave us alone, Abby. I think Kitty is very angry with me. I'm afraid she will not listen to me."

After ringing the bell for Healy, Abby resumed her seat, almost as nervous as Peter. Although she knew Kitty loved Peter, her reaction was unpredictable.

"You wanted to see me, Abby?" Kitty asked, her normal vivacity dampened since she had vowed to forget Peter.

"We have a visitor, Kitty."

Kitty spun round, some sixth sense warning her of the identity of the third person. Composing herself, she said coolly, "Good day, Lord Abbott."

Her formal address caused the other two to exchange speaking glances. Abby motioned for everyone to be seated and took charge of the conversation. "Kitty, dear, you will remember that Peter offered for you before we moved to Town for the Season, but we all agreed that the two of you needed a little Town bronze to be sure of your choice."

"A wise decision, as it turns out, Abby, since Lord Abbott has become enamoured of Miss Pilling," Kitty said stiffly.

"Stop it!" Peter exploded, jumping up from his chair. "You know that is not true, Kitty! And do not call me 'Lord Abbott' as though we were strangers."

"But we *are* strangers! You are not Peter. You are a man-about-Town who escorts other young ladies to social events."

"Only once, Kitty. And that was Willie's idea," Peter said miserably.

"I should have known," Kitty murmured. "Then you have no tendre for Miss Pilling?"

"None at all. But I barely escaped offering for her after your mischief-making last evening!"

"I did nothing!"

"Yes, you did. You—"

"Children, please. Kitty, Peter has come here today to ask me to now consider his suit, and I have agreed, if it is still your wish to marry him."

Kitty looked from Abby to Peter in shock. "You—you do not object, Abby?"

"No, love, I don't. I believe you truly care for each other. And you have both had an opportunity to meet others."

"And you are sure you are not offering for me because you feel obligated?" the young lady asked, her large blue eyes searching the face of the young man who stood across the room from her.

With swift movement, Peter fell to one knee in front of her, lifting her hand to his lips. "It is my greatest desire, dear heart. I have missed you so much."

"Oh, Peter," Kitty whispered, her hand caressing his cheek.

Abby rose and slipped from the room, her presence no longer needed.

ABBY MET MARY as she came up the stairs. "Hello, my love. Did you enjoy your ride with Mr. Morrison?"

"Yes, of course," Mary said glumly.

Taking her sister's arm, Abby walked her upstairs to her bedroom. "Peter just arrived to ask again for Kitty's hand," she said lightly as they entered Mary's room.

Mary's interest was awakened. "Did you give it?"

"Yes, of course. I am only glad he persisted."

"Oh, I am so grateful, Abby," Mary said, hugging her oldest sister. "They are perfect for each other."

"Yes, their reunion was quite touching." Abby hesitated before saying slowly, "Mary, I have been thinking. I believe it would be a mistake for you to marry where your heart is not engaged. You do not care for Mr. Morrison, do you?"

Mary moved away from her sister, fingering the bed hangings. "No," she said in a low voice. "I have come to the same conclusion, Abby. I tried so hard this afternoon, but I could not bring myself to..."

"It is all right, love," Abby consoled her sister, hugging her. "If you wish, we can come again next Season. Our finances are in good order."

Smiling weakly, Mary said, "Perhaps. I will admit that I am ready to retire to the country for now. The Season has been more fatiguing than I expected."

"It is your heart that is tired, my dear, as is mine. But we will recover."

"Yes, Abby." But she did not sound convinced of it.

MR. RUSSELL WAS QUITE PLEASED with himself as he descended to dinner. He had enjoyed his afternoon and was looking forward to seeing Miss Milhouse that evening. He felt sure this time she would dance with him.

He entered the library, where he and his cousin met before dinner each evening, with a smile on his face. In contrast, his cousin was sprawled in a chair, a drink already in his hand. He was frowning at the fireplace as if it offended him. A closer observation convinced Mr. Russell that was not his cousin's first drink, by any means.

"Good evening, Richard. How was your day?"

Lord Harrington stared at his cousin before slapping his glass down on a side-table. "My day was excellent! Why do you ask?"

Mr. Russell moved over to pour himself a sherry, watching his cousin from the corner of his eye. "No reason."

"Well, I had a fine day," Lord Harrington slurred. "I did not want to join that insipid parade in the Park, anyway."

"Oh? I thought you had planned to escort Miss Mary Milhouse."

"She excused herself. Said she had discussed it with her sister and there was no longer any need for me to escort her."

Mr. Russell stared at his cousin's gloomy face as he tried to fathom the meaning of his statement. "Did you invite Miss Mary to drive with you for a reason other than the pleasure of her company?"

"Yes. No. I don't know." Lord Harrington picked up his glass and drank deeply.

"What other reason would you have?" Mr. Russell asked curiously.

"We were planning your marriage." Lord Harrington focussed his eyes momentarily. "Wasn't sh-supposed to tell you that."

"I won't give you away," Mr. Russell said gently. "But why would Miss Mary be concerned about my marriage?"

"Because her sister was to be the bride, of course. Only now, I guess you will have to remain a widower."

"I'm afraid you are right. You see, I was considering Miss Milhouse, but I did not want to take on the task of finding husbands for all her sisters. It would be too formidable a chore." Mr. Russell watched his cousin's reaction.

"Don't see why. Good-looking family. Besides, it'd only be two sisters. You know Norfolk is going to marry Miss Phoebe Milhouse."

"Even better, Miss Kitty Milhouse is going to marry Lord Abbott. That only leaves Miss Mary Milhouse."

"One sister shouldn't stop you," Lord Harrington said, sitting up straighter.

"I do not know. Miss Mary is a nice girl, but not as pretty as the other two."

"She is intelligent and sensitive and kind and . . . and a darling," Lord Harrington finished dreamily.

"You are right. And I believe a certain Mr. Morrison may be brought up to scratch."

"What?" Lord Harrington roared.

"When I arrived at their residence today to talk to Miss Milhouse, Mr. Morrison was escorting Miss Mary for a ride in the Park. His manner was most possessive."

"That was *my* ride in the Park," Lord Harrington protested bitterly. "She does not know what she is doing. He will never be able to make her happy. He is a . . . a toad-eater with no future."

"Oh, well, Miss Mary must marry someone. It might as well be Mr. Morrison," Mr. Russell said casually, his eyes trained on his cousin from under lowered lids.

"No! No! It should be me! I can take care of her, make her happy. She wants to have children," he said more softly. "They should be *my* children," he finished, staring far away, a slight smile on his face.

"So why have you not asked for her hand in marriage? Why have you not told her you care for her?"

Lord Harrington sank back into his chair and covered his face with his hands. "I do not know. I think . . . I am afraid."

Mr. Russell put his hand on his cousin's shoulder. "You have never been a coward, Richard. Of what are you afraid?"

"It is absurd," Lord Harrington said with a mirthless laugh. "I have been pursued by many husband-hunting young ladies. I know I am considered a catch, but . . . I care for Mary. I want to be her husband, her protector. I want her to love me." He paused, drawing a deep breath, before looking up at his cousin with beseeching eyes. "What if she does not?"

Squeezing his cousin's shoulder, Mr. Russell said, "There are several wise sayings I could offer you, Richard, but I suspect you would not appreciate them at this moment." He moved over to sit down in front of Lord Harrington. "You will have to decide what to do. Of course," Mr. Russell offered with a chuckle, "I could always approach Miss Milhouse for you."

Lord Harrington leaned forward eagerly, shedding the lethargy brought on by despair and alcohol. "Could you, Giles? I would not ask it, but . . ."

"I will gladly talk with her, Richard, but if you have not given any indication of your feelings to the young lady, her sister may know nothing of *her* feelings."

"When will you talk with her?"

The eagerness Lord Harrington demonstrated was a repetition of that shown by Lord Norfolk and Lord Abbott. "I seem to have established a tradition of discussing these matters while driving in Hyde Park. I believe I shall invite Miss Milhouse to join me in another drive tomorrow."

LATE THAT EVENING, the two men returned to their residence.

"Where do you think they were?" Lord Harrington asked tiredly. "We attended every possible soirée, musicale and ball, and they were nowhere to be seen."

"No, they were not. But could you believe Lady Jeffrey's lemon cake was served at at least half of those entertainments?"

"I hope I never see another piece of that devilish cake. Why do you suppose it is so popular? It can't be the way it tastes," Lord Harrington said in disgust.

"You do not know?" Mr. Russell asked in amusement.

"Know what?"

"Lady Jeffrey's cake is said to be a love potion."

Lord Harrington stopped in his progress up the front steps, his eyes wide with shock. "You cannot be serious!"

"That is the rumour circulating among the ton. It is not true, of course, but desperate Mamas will try anything."

The men moved up the stairs again. As the door was opened to them by Bates, Lord Harrington muttered, "I wonder if Mary has eaten any of her aunt's cake."

THE NOTE FROM Mr. Russell arrived the next morning while Abby was at the breakfast table.

"Why would Mr. Russell write you?" Kitty asked. She was in a sunny mood after her reconciliation with Peter. The family had celebrated the night before with a quiet dinner which included Lord Norfolk. Abby had had a private meeting with the older man before dinner, accepting him into the family as well as Peter.

"It is probably something about Jonathan. I am sorry he was not here to join us last evening. He will be delighted to be no longer the only male in the family."

"Is he due back this afternoon?" Mary asked.

"Yes, I believe—" Abby stopped as she perused Mr. Russell's note, a frown on her face.

"Is anything wrong?" Mary asked, drawing the others' attention to Abby.

"No, no, nothing is wrong," Abby said, hurriedly refolding her letter, as if afraid someone might read its contents. She rose from her chair. "I must—must see to the day's menus," she said as she slipped from the room.

Instead of descending to Mrs. Healy's room, Abby slipped up the stairs and into her bedchamber, closing the door behind her. She sank into the chair by her window and took out the letter to re-read it.

Dear Miss Milhouse,
I beg your presence for a drive in Hyde Park today at three. I have much that will interest you, including a message from Jonathan. And remember, I promised you my best.

Yours,
Giles Russell

Her fingers reached out and traced the signature. It was her first letter from Mr. Russell . . . and probably her last. What did he mean by "his best"? Surely it could not be another proposal? Unless . . . could it be that Lord Harrington had an interest in Mary? It would be marvellous, but she had thought that yesterday and been wrong.

Ah, well, better to not get her hopes up. And she certainly would say nothing to Mary. But it wouldn't hurt to look her best when she took her drive with Mr. Russell.

When Abby returned downstairs to the parlour, she was dressed in her favorite lilac gown, her hair arranged in soft curls.

"You look wonderful, Abby," Mary enthused, her eyes searching her sister's face. She had been afraid the note from Mr. Russell had upset her sister.

"Thank you, my love. I am going for a ride with Mr. Russell today."

Kitty looked up. "You have been driving out with Mr. Russell quite often, have you not?"

"Perhaps Abby will be receiving a proposal soon, also," Phoebe chipped in.

Noting Mary's brave smile, Abby said, "I do not think so, Phoebe. Mr. Russell has asked me to drive with him on behalf of Lord Norfolk, Peter and now Jonathan. He said in his note he had a message from Jonathan."

Healy opened the door to announced Mr. Morrison. Mary flashed a panicky look at Abby.

"Good day, Mr. Morrison," Abby said as the man entered the room.

"Good day, Miss Milhouse, ladies," the man said genially before moving across the room to sit down beside Mary.

Abby was grateful she and Mary had discussed her intentions towards this man before now. He would not fit in with their family.

The door opened again to admit Lady Jeffrey. After greeting her nieces and Mr. Morrison, she settled down with her bag of knitting, a pleased smile on her face. "How nice of you to call, Mr. Morrison. Abby, have you not sent for the tea tray? And be sure there is some of my special cake on it for Mr. Morrison.''

Abby ignored Mary's pleading eyes and rang for Healy, relaying her aunt's request. It didn't matter how much lemon cake Mr. Morrison ate. Mary would not accept his offer, thank goodness. When she returned to her seat, Mr. Morrison was expounding on a bill his employer had introduced in the House of Lords. According to Mr. Morrison, the impetus for such action stemmed from his own social conscience.

The pomposity of his remarks left his listeners glassy-eyed. Relief was universal when Healy arrived with the tea tray. Several lighter topics were introduced by Kitty and Mary, but Mr. Morrison returned to his self-promotion each time they took a breath.

The arrival of both Lord Norfolk and Peter rescued Phoebe and Kitty from Mr. Morrison's monologue, but it left Mary, Abby and Lady Jeffrey still trapped. When the two couples rose to join the daily parade in the Park, Abby hoped Mr. Morrison would take his leave. He had already overstayed the thirty minutes dictated by Society for a visit.

Mr. Morrison, instead, asked for a private interview with Abby. After exchanging a pained look with Mary, who restated with her eyes her answer to the obvious question, Abby agreed politely to his request, leading him to the library.

It was not a pleasant interview. Mr. Morrison insisted Mary had misled him, but Abby steadfastly refused his demand that Mary be affianced to him. The only thing for which she was grateful was the fact that Mr. Morrison did not have a single romantic bone in his body.

Abby returned to the parlour to find Mr. Russell waiting patiently, chatting with Lady Jeffrey and Mary. Abby smiled warmly into Mary's concerned eyes, hoping to relieve her of her worry. Then she turned to greet Mr. Russell. "Good day. I'm sorry I kept you waiting, Mr. Russell."

"I have enjoyed my visit with these charming ladies, Miss Milhouse."

"But I cannot persuade him to taste my lemon cake, Abby," Lady Jeffrey complained with a grin. "He accused me of trying to snag him for one of you girls. I told him he'd have to hurry. You're about the only one left after today."

Both Abby and Mary turned crimson while Mr. Russell lifted an enquiring eyebrow.

"If your are ready, Mr. Russell, I'll just fetch my bonnet and shawl," Abby said hurriedly.

"I await your pleasure, Miss Milhouse," Mr. Russell responded with a half bow. His face gave no indication of his thoughts, but inside Mr. Russell was wondering if he had arrived too late to plead his cousin's suit.

Abby hurried to her room, afraid of what else Aunt Bea would say in her absence. In no time at all, she was seated in Mr. Russell's high-perch phaeton on the way to Hyde Park.

MR. RUSSELL MAINTAINED QUIET until they entered the Park, but once they had joined the parade, he could no longer control his fears.

Abruptly he said, "Did Miss Mary receive a proposal this morning?" At Abby's raised eyebrows, he said, "I know I should not ask such a question, but it is important I know the answer."

Staring straight ahead, Abby said quietly, "Mary did receive an offer, but . . . but it was rejected."

Mr. Russell said nothing and Abby felt compelled to explain. "She intended to accept it because . . . she wants to marry and have a family, but she could not bring herself to enter into a marriage where her heart had no interest.''

"That is not considered important by the members of the ton, Miss Milhouse.''

"I know. But my parents had that kind of marriage, loving each other and sharing their lives. And that is what I want for all of my sisters. I am grateful for your assistance in finding that kind of marriage for Phoebe and Kitty.''

"And Mary?''

"I do not want Mary to settle for second best. I love all my sisters, Mr. Russell, but Mary . . . Mary is special. She is bright, loving, loyal . . .''

"Someone recently described her as a darling.''

Abby's eyes flew to Mr. Russell's face.

"No, it was not me. I am certainly an admirer of Miss Mary, but my heart is not involved.''

Abby's own heart fluttered in relief.

"I promised you I would do my best, and I believe I have. For the third time, my dear Miss Milhouse, I come to you with an offer of marriage for the last of your unmarried sisters.''

CHAPTER SIXTEEN

ABBY'S HEART RACED at his words. "Who—"

"My cousin, of course. He has given his heart to Miss Mary and is fearful she will have none of him."

"You are sure, Mr. Russell? I know they have spent much time together, but it was not—" Abby broke off as she realized where her words had taken her.

Mr. Russell noted her rosy cheeks but did not allude to her unfinished statement. "I think for a time Richard believed he sought her company for other reasons. But before too long, he only used it as an excuse to be with Miss Mary. She is perfect for him. Not only is she attractive, but also intelligent, and she shares his interest in the unusual."

"Yes, I have often thought what a wonderful couple they would make. But I was not sure Lord Harrington...that is, he could choose among all the debutantes, the rich, the beautiful...Mary's portion is respectable but not large."

"That does not matter. Richard is quite wealthy. And among all those rich and beautiful young women, he has discovered the perfect one for him."

Abby closed her eyes in a silent prayer of gratitude. Of all her sisters, Mary deserved the best, but life did not always grant its riches to the deserving.

"My cousin would have approached you himself, but he feared Miss Mary did not hold him in high regard. It seems he has not given her any indication of his feelings."

"No, I do not believe he has." In her joy, Abby felt light-hearted, but Mr. Russell's serious mien brought her giddiness under control. "I believe my sister would welcome a proposal from Lord Harrington, Mr. Russell, though, of course, she must speak for herself."

Seeing the delight in her eyes, Mr. Russell nodded. "Good." They drove on, acknowledging the greetings of other members of the ton. After a moment, Mr. Russell said, "Well, it appears we shall be related, Miss Milhouse."

Abby cast him a startled glance. "I beg your pardon?"

"When my cousin—pardon me, I should say *if* my cousin marries your sister, she will be my cousin-in-law. Since you are her sister, we shall be related."

"Perhaps a distant connection," Abby said with a smile. "Hardly relations, Mr. Russell."

"At least allow Thomas and Jonathan to consider themselves cousins. They will be thrilled."

"True," Abby agreed, chuckling. "I can never thank you enough for allowing Jonathan to join Thomas in his studies. Jonathan has never been happier. In fact, the success of our Season has depended on you, Mr. Russell. You have befriended strangers in a most amazing way."

"You do not seem strangers to me, Miss Milhouse. In fact, I feel a most proprietorial interest in your family."

"Ah, now, perhaps. But I remember your first visit. You did not appear best pleased to be there."

Mr. Russell chuckled. "Well, truthfully, I was not. It was my first venture back into Society, forced upon me by my cousin. And I found myself surrounded by four beautiful young ladies. It was a frightening experience."

"Really, Mr. Russell," Abby scoffed, "you try my intelligence with such a tale. You did not appear the least bit frightened."

"I hide my emotions well," he assured her humbly.

Unable to hold back a laugh, Abby concurred, "You must, sir, if you were trembling in your boots that day."

"Frankly, after your aunt's performance with the lemon cake, I was a little uneasy."

"And I was horrified. I did not then know what she was up to. It was only later that she confessed her belief about the cake."

Before Mr. Russell could respond, they were hailed by Lord Norfolk and Phoebe. "Good day. You are in good looks, Miss Phoebe," Mr. Russell greeted them.

"Thank you, sir. Abby, Jason has just suggested that we visit his estate, the entire family, this next week. Would that not be delightful?"

"That is most kind of you, Lord Norfolk," Abby said, smiling at the gentleman. "We must consult with Aunt Bea and your sisters, Phoebe."

"Yes, Abby. Have you seen Kitty and Peter? They are having one of their famous arguments about someone's horse."

"Oh, dear, is Kitty causing a scene?"

"No, not really. And she is enjoying herself."

"Yes, she always does when they argue, especially since she and Peter are reconciled."

"She is not drawing undue attention to herself, Miss Milhouse. Lord Abbott has her well in hand," Lord Norfolk assured Abby quietly.

Both Mr. Russell and Abby raised their eyebrows. "Perhaps visiting London has improved Peter's ability to deal with Kitty," Abby said in wonder.

Everyone laughed at her expression. "Perhaps her sister was wise in suggesting a Season for both of them," Mr. Russell commented with a warm smile for his companion.

"Shall we see you this evening at the theatre, Giles?" Lord Norfolk asked. "I am escorting the Milhouse ladies."

"Then you may be assured you shall see me, Norfolk," Mr. Russell replied, "as well as my cousin."

"Good. We must be on our way. My bays do not like to stand."

Mr. Russell put his vehicle into motion. "I did not know you were to go to the theatre this evening."

"Lord Norfolk invited us last evening."

"What entertainment did you attend? We looked for you but you were nowhere to be seen."

"We had a family dinner to welcome Lord Norfolk and Peter into our family. I hated that Jonathan was not—I forgot. You said you had a message from Jonathan."

"Yes. My man of business needed another day or two on the estate and Jonathan asked if you would mind if he stayed. He is having a wonderful time."

"I'm sure he is, but is he not in the way?"

"No, not at all. As I'm sure you know, Thomas is much less trouble when he has Jonathan with him than when he is alone. They have become as close as brothers."

"Yes," Abby said with a sigh. "I'm afraid Jonathan will be lonesome when we return to our estate. But yes, of course, he may remain as long as is necessary."

WHEN MR. RUSSELL RETURNED Abby to her home, he assisted her down from his phaeton and walked her up to the door. "I shall see you this evening. I believe Norfolk will allow me to join the party."

Abby frowned. Finally she looked up at Mr. Russell with worried grey eyes. "Mr. Russell, I always enjoy your company, but since we have been seen together so often of late, I'm afraid we may cause talk." Before he could speak, she hurried on. "I, of course, understand that you have no—that is, that our meetings have been for particular reasons, but the ton might not. I think it would be best if we were not seen together for . . . for a while." She whirled round and entered the door Healy had opened before Giles Russell could protest.

He proceeded at once to his own town house to inform his cousin of Miss Milhouse's favourable response, all the while making some plans of his own.

ONCE HE HAD HEARD the news, Lord Harrington, tormented by the wait, immediately returned to his own house to put his fortune to the touch. Abby had calmly rejoined her aunt and Mary, explaining to them why Jonathan would not be returning that afternoon, but saying nothing about the other part of their conversation. When Healy entered the drawing-room and informed her that Lord Harrington desired a private interview with her, she rose and left the room without ever meeting Mary's enquiring stare.

"Good day, Lord Harrington," Abby said as she entered the library where Healy had left the gentleman.

"Good day, Miss Milhouse." He grinned foolishly as he said, "I daresay you know why I have come. Giles said—that is—I am asking for Mary's hand in marriage."

Abby smiled but only said, "Why do you wish to marry her, my lord?"

Surprised at such an unusual question, Lord Harrington stumbled over his answer. "Why, I . . . she is intelligent, and lovely, and . . . I care for her very deeply."

"Then I have no objection to your proposal, my lord," Abby said. "In fact, I am delighted. But I would prefer that Mary give you her decision, as I have not discussed the possibility of such a marriage with her." Because she did not believe it could ever happen, Abby thought with joy. Rising, followed by Lord Harrington jumping to his feet, Abby rang for Healy who appeared immediately. "Send Miss Mary to us, please, Healy."

Lord Harrington offered to discuss settlements with Abby, but she suggested they wait until after his interview with Mary, thereby increasing his nervousness.

Mary entered the library apprehensively. She was afraid to hope her dreams might have come true. But she could think of no other reason for what was happening.

Abby kissed her sister on her cheek before saying, "My dear, Lord Harrington would like to ask you something. I will return in a few minutes."

Mary stared after her sister, only turning back to Lord Harrington when he nervously cleared his throat.

"Yes, my lord?"

"Won't you be seated, Mary?" He gestured to the leather couch, and Mary sat down gingerly at one end of it.

His throat dry and his limbs shaky, Lord Harrington joined her there and reached out to take her hand in his. "Mary... Mary, ever since I arrived home and discovered your family in residence, I have been impressed with your dignity, your intelligence, your warmth. And... and I would like you to be the mother of my children."

"I'm afraid I could not do that, my lord," Mary said calmly.

"Why not?" Lord Harrington demanded, none too pleased with her response.

"It would not be proper to have children outside of marriage."

Lord Harrington was stunned. It was not until he saw the merry twinkle in her eye that he remembered Mary had a wicked sense of humour. "Mary, I shall beat you five times a day. How could you do that to me?"

"What, my lord?"

"Do not sit there all calm and teasing! You know I meant marriage! It is unladylike of you to even suggest I meant otherwise."

"I would not presume such a thing. I only know what you have told me, and there was no mention of marriage."

Though he wanted to take her in his arms, Lord Harrington slipped from the couch onto one knee in front of the young lady.

"My dear Miss Mary Milhouse, will you do me the nonour of becoming my wife?"

Mary reached out a hand to cup his cheek as she solemnly said, "It is my greatest desire." Before Lord Harrington could respond, however, Mary said, "But I must warn you of one thing, my lord."

He frowned but waited for her to continue. Ducking her head so he could not see her face clearly, she said in a low voice, "I think it only fair to tell you that—that it will not be a marriage of convenience for me."

A flame flickered in his green eyes and he said softly, "Are you saying our marriage will be inconvenient, my dear?"

Mary, never a coward, lifted her pale blue eyes to his to whisper, "Most inconvenient, my lord. You see, I love you."

In a flicker of an eyelash, Lord Harrington had scooped his fiancée from the couch and settled himself in her place, with Mary in his lap. "You deserve a reward for your honesty, my love," he said gently before caressing her soft lips with his. When Mary's instinctively clung, Lord Harrington deepened the kiss, his arms tightening about her.

He drew back from Mary's glowing face, her eyes closed, and sent a silent prayer of thanks that he had remained a bachelor until now. "Mary, my dear, you must open your eyes, or I will think I have harmed you."

Her eyelids fluttered open and a beatific smile lit her face. "Harm, my lord? I think you have found the cure to all ills."

"Do you think you could call me Richard? It seems ridiculous to remain so formal after that kiss."

"I will try to remember," Mary said primly, but her eyes twinkled up at him.

"In case my actions have not told you, sweet Mary, I will be inconvenienced by our marriage also, because I love you to distraction."

There was another celebration that exceeded the first in taking Mary's breath away. When she had somewhat recovered, she murmured, "You are sure?"

"Quite sure," Lord Harrington said drily. "When you said Mr. Morrison would be the father of your children, I was ready to call him out at dawn."

"*Our* children will be much more beautiful. They will have auburn hair, like their father, and be strong and tall."

"Then for their sake, I devoutly hope they are all sons. Can we not have some delightful daughters like their mother?"

Mary chuckled and snuggled into his shoulder. Before she could answer, however, the sound of footsteps required an adjustment to their positions.

Abby opened the door with a greeting, knowing no question was necessary about Mary's answer. However, their faces would have told her had she not felt confident of Mary's acceptance of his offer. "Congratulations, Lord Harrington. It appears you have been successful in your suit."

Standing, he offered his hand to his future sister-in-law, a large grin on his face. "Beyond my wildest dreams, Miss Milhouse. I hope your family will welcome me into their midst."

"Certainly. All we desire is Mary's happiness, and I believe it lies with you."

"And perhaps all of you could bring yourselves to call me Richard when we are family?"

"I daresay we could manage...Richard," Abby said with a grin. "Now, perhaps you will join us in the drawing-room. Everyone but Jonathan is present and you may share your good news with them."

WHEN LORD HARRINGTON returned to his cousin's house late that afternoon, he was enchanted with life. Such happiness had never been his until his Mary had entered his life. Eager to share his feelings with his cousin, he found him in the library with Lord Norfolk and Lord Abbott.

"Oh, sorry, Giles. I'll talk to you later."

"No, Richard, I need you now. You know Lord Norfolk and Lord Abbott, I believe."

"Certainly. And since we are to be related, I'm sure I will soon know them better."

Congratulations were extended to Lord Harrington and he joined the other men, pleased with life.

"As I was just telling these two gentlemen, when I assisted each of you with your suit for the hand of one of the Misses Milhouse, you expressed gratitude and an offer to assist me in any way possible. I'm afraid I must call in those debts now."

The offers, given in a moment of ecstasy, would never be denied, but each of the gentlemen wondered what they would be called upon to do.

"Nothing so very terrible," Mr. Russell assured them. "I, too, intend to become a member of this remarkable family. It is my greatest hope that Miss Milhouse will accept my offer of marriage."

Congratulations were offered by all three men, but Mr. Russell refused to accept them. "She has not agreed to my offer. In matter of fact, I have not made it. But unless I intend to do so in public, I'm not sure I will have the opportunity. That is where you three come in."

The others listened to Mr. Russell's plan and each pledged their assistance.

AT THE THEATRE that evening, Abby and Lady Jeffrey sat in the back of Lord Norfolk's box, observing the three young couples in front of them.

"It has turned out well, hasn't it, Aunt Bea?" Abby said with a sigh.

"You have done well, my dear," Lady Jeffrey agreed, "but I would like to see you as happy as the other three. You are a good girl and deserve better than life with an old lady and a young boy."

"Nonsense, Aunt Bea. I am most fortunate to have your company and support. And I would not be without Jonathan. It is almost as if he is my own child rather than my brother."

"I know, love, but—"

"Ssh, the curtain is rising," Abby said in relief.

AT INTERMISSION, Mary turned to talk to her sister. "Abby, Richard wondered if we would like to drive down to Riverview, Mr. Russell's estate, and fetch Jonathan home tomorrow. He said it is a pleasant two-hour drive from London. Mr. Russell has offered to have his chef prepare a nuncheon for us."

"Are you sure Mr. Russell would not mind us invading his estate, Mary? We have depended on his goodness too often since our move to London."

"Giles does not mind, Miss Milhouse," Lord Harrington assured her. "We will do him a favour by returning Thomas as well. Mr. Wilson has run into some difficulties and cannot bring the boys back."

"In that case, we will, of course, be willing to do so. I am delighted to have the opportunity to repay him in some small way for his kindnesses."

"A day in the country sounds delightful, doesn't it, Kitty?" Lord Abbott said enthusiastically. "May we join you?"

"Well, of course, if Lord Harrington does not think it would make too much work for Mr. Russell's staff?"

"Of course not. Why don't you and Miss Phoebe join us, too, Norfolk?"

Though Phoebe was not enthusiastic about a long carriage ride and a day spent in the country, her fiancé gave her no opportunity to decline. "We'd be delighted. It will be a family outing."

In no time at all, their day was planned.

ABBY WAS HAPPY Jonathan would be returning with them, but she was not too pleased about spending the day at Mr. Russell's estate. At least he would not be joining them, she thought as she tied her new bonnet under her chin. It would have been a more enjoyable day for her if he came, but she must become adjusted to doing without his intoxicating company. After all, she had no more sisters available for matrimony.

Abby discovered the rest of her family waiting in the parlour with Lord Abbott and Lord Norfolk. Only Lord Harrington was missing.

"Is everyone ready?" she asked gaily.

"Do you know, I don't believe I shall accompany you," Aunt Bea said. She was dressed in a deep-purple walking dress, prepared for an outing.

"Why ever not, Aunt Bea?" Abby asked at once.

"I have received a note from Alice Carouthers, asking me to call. She has not been feeling well. You will be sufficient chaperon for a family outing, Abby. Would you mind terribly if I did not go?"

"Of course not, Aunt Bea. We shall manage."

"Good," Lady Jeffrey said, patting her reticule with delight. In truth, she had received a note, but it was not from Mrs. Carouthers.

"Lord Harrington is below, Miss Abby," Healy announced. "Shall he come up, or is everyone ready to depart?"

"We are ready, Healy," Norfolk said, pulling Phoebe up from her seat. "Shall we go down?"

Abby was surprised to have Lord Norfolk take charge, but she had no quarrel with his decision. She joined the others after placing a kiss on Lady Jeffrey's cheek.

"Enjoy yourself, my dear," Lady Jeffrey had whispered.

When she reached the front steps, the last of their party, she discovered there had been a change in their number. Two laudalets were standing down below, two couples in one and one in the other.

In front of those carriages was a familiar rig. Mr. Russell was standing beside his high-perch phaeton, talking to Lord Harrington. When he saw her, he broke off his speech and came up the steps to meet her.

"Good morning, Miss Milhouse. I hope you do not mind that I have decided to join the party. I need to speak with Mr. Wilson concerning several things."

"No, of course not, Mr. Russell. After all, it is your estate," Abby said with a frown.

"Good. Will you give me company in my phaeton? I do not relish the thought of driving the distance alone."

Abby looked at her sisters and their fiancés and then back to Mr. Russell. "If you wish it, certainly."

"With all my heart," Mr. Russell said with a warm smile that sent shivers down Miss Milhouse's neck.

She allowed him to assist her to her seat in his phaeton. Just as he sprang up to join her, she heard Mary exclaim, "Oh, dear, I have forgotten my sketch pad. May I just return to fetch it?"

Lord Harrington immediately assisted his fiancée down from the laudalet. Then he assured the others they would only be a moment.

Mr. Russell called out to his cousin as he mounted the stairs, "We shall begin our journey. My horses do not stand well. We shall see you at Riverview."

Before Abby could even think of objecting, she found her residence left behind. She felt uneasy about the events of the morning, but it was beyond her control to change any of it. With a sigh, she vowed to enjoy this last outing in Mr. Russell's company.

CHAPTER SEVENTEEN

THE WEATHER was exceedingly pleasant and, once they were outside London, the scenery enjoyable. Abby relaxed and chatted with Mr. Russell on many subjects. They compared notes on their own childhoods and those of Jonathan and Thomas. There was a friendly argument on the finer points of child-rearing and remarks on the changes occurring in the Milhouse family.

As usual when in Mr. Russell's company, time passed with amazing ease, and Abby was surprised when Mr. Russell slowed the pace of his horses.

"Are we to Riverview already?" she asked in surprise.

"Almost. I thought we might take some repose while waiting for the others. I brought along some refreshments in case we grew thirsty on the way."

He pulled the phaeton to a halt alongside a stream which gurgled through a green meadow. Jumping down, Mr. Russell reached under his seat and drew forth a basket. From that he took a coverlet and spread it on the grass beneath a large oak tree. Then he returned to the carriage to assist Miss Milhouse to the ground.

"It has been such a pleasant drive. How convenient to have an estate so near London."

"Yes, it is. I have several others, but they are much farther away. Therefore, we visit them less often."

Abby settled down on the cover, spreading her skirts around her. She breathed deeply of the clear country air.

"I am anxious to see Jonathan again. I miss him, even though he is noisy."

"That happens to be a most endearing quality in you, Miss Milhouse."

"What? That I miss my brother?"

"No. That you, an elegant young woman, give time and care to your brother. Most debutantes I have met give little thought to anything but their own comfort."

Abby smiled wryly. "But there is your mistake, Mr. Russell. I am not a debutante. It is a very time-consuming occupation, being a debutante. Everyone expects you to look beautiful and be pleasant every minute of the day. As a chaperon, I am allowed my off days."

"I have as yet to see one, Miss Milhouse. You always appear to advantage, and you also demonstrate the patience of a saint with your family."

"Please, Mr. Russell, you are putting me to the blush. I will be compelled to confess all my sins if you continue in such a manner."

He smiled as he removed a jug of lemonade from the basket along with two glasses. "I doubt you would convince me of your unworthiness, my dear." Handing her a glass of lemonade, he ignored her protests.

Abby sipped her drink and glanced around the grassy knoll on which they were seated. She was uncomfortable being the subject of their conversation.

Mr. Russell watched his companion with loving eyes. She was such a charming young lady, kind, modest and intelligent. As he reached back into the basket, he said, "Miss Milhouse, there is something I must ask you, but first you must have something to relieve your hunger."

"I am not at all sharp set, Mr. Russell. Please, what is it? Is it something about Jonathan? Oh dear, I should have known," she said with a shaky laugh. "I have no more sisters whose suitors would have importuned your intervention, so it must be Jonathan.''

"No, it is not Jonathan," Mr. Russell said calmly as he handed his companion a delicate china saucer and a fork. "Please, Miss Milhouse, eat."

Abby had taken the plate without looking at it, her eyes searching Mr. Russell's face for some indication of the problem. Now she automatically picked up her fork. The sooner she ate, the sooner she would know the problem. Looking down, however, brought her to an abrupt stillness.

Finally she looked at Mr. Russell, a frown on her face. "Lemon cake, Mr. Russell?"

"Lemon cake, Miss Milhouse," he assured her with a pleased smile.

"You are not having any?"

"I do not need it."

"Nor do I, sir," Abby said, still puzzled.

"Oh, yes, you do, my dear."

"I do not understand. Why—" she paused as a horrible thought struck her. "Mr. Russell, if my aunt asked you to find me a husband, you must disregard her, please. She has a silly bee in her bonnet about my marrying, but, truly..."

"Your aunt has suggested no such thing."

His calm manner and pleasant smile left Abby in confusion. "Then I still do not understand why you have served me lemon cake."

"I am beginning to despair of you, Abigail Milhouse. First you assume I only seek your company because of others, and now you refuse to eat the special love potion I have provided. How will I ever convince you to marry me if you do not eat the lemon cake?''

Abby's eyes grew round as she listened to his explanation, shining with joy as he finished. "You might take an old-fashioned approach, sir, such as asking me. I have heard it is most efficacious."

Mr. Russell took the plate from her hands and placed it on the cover. Then he knelt beside her with both her hands in his and said softly, "Will you marry me, Miss Milhouse?"

"Are you asking me to marry you because I will be a good mother for Thomas?" she asked, her eyes concentrated on their clasped hands.

"Yes."

Abby's eyes flashed up to his before dropping again. "And will you allow Jonathan and Aunt Bea to reside with us, at least until Jonathan is of age?"

"Of course. We will need Aunt Bea to provide the lemon cake," he said solemnly.

"Why will we have need of lemon cake?"

"So that when we bring our many daughters to London for their Seasons, we may snag them a rich husband just by serving lemon cake."

Noting his broad smile, Abby asked, "What if we only have sons?"

"Then we shall become wealthy making lemon cake for all the desperate Mamas with spotty daughters in need of a husband."

Abby laughed but then quietly asked, "Do you truly wish to marry me, Mr. Russell?"

"I do truly wish to marry you, my darling Miss Milhouse, more than anything in the world."

"I—I truly wish to marry you also, but . . ."

"What is it, my love?" Mr. Russell asked as he sat down beside her and brazenly placed his arm about her. Abby discovered that her head fit naturally into the curve of his shoulder.

"I do not think your first marriage was a happy one. And—and I thought you did not intend to remarry."

Mr. Russell lightly kissed her temple, breathing in the flowery scent she always wore. "You are right, my love. My first marriage was bearable, at best. And I did not intend to remarry until I was faced with such an incomparable specimen as yourself."

"Please, do not tease. I do not want to marry you if it will make you unhappy, even for the boys' sake."

Pulling her around to face him, Mr. Russell took her face in his hands. "Listen to me, my little love. I am not marrying you for Thomas, or for Jonathan, or even for Aunt Bea. And I am not marrying you because I ate too much lemon cake. I swear I never tasted it. I am marrying you because I will be unhappy the rest of my life if you are not by my side. Because I want to have more children, little girls who look like you, little boys who look like me. Or the other way round. I do not care as long as you are their mother. Please, will you marry me?"

"Oh, yes, please!" Abby exclaimed before she could speak no more. Mr. Russell ended their conversation in the most satisfactory way possible.

SOME TIME LATER, when Mr. Russell poured them both more lemonade to toast their engagement, Abby became aware that quite a lot of time had passed and the others had not yet arrived. "Do you suppose something has happened?"

"Why, no, I expect them to arrive right on schedule."

Something in his voice alerted Abby to an irregularity. She was already learning to read her future husband. "What are you hiding from me, Giles?"

His innocent look crumbled into laughter. "Oh, my sweet Abby. I shall never be able to hide anything from you, shall I? You are much too clever by half."

"And you have not yet told me why the others have not arrived."

Taking her back into his arms and saluting her perception with a deep kiss, he presently said, "They have not yet arrived because I invited them for supper. They never left Town. Instead, they all returned home and packed for several days, and this afternoon they will set out on their drive, arriving here about five o'clock."

"But . . . how did you manage to plan such a thing?"

"I collected my debts. The three gentlemen soon to become members of your family had offered to assist me whenever I had need, so I took advantage of their offers. And they, in turn, convinced your sisters that you would be pleased with the opportunity to visit your new home with me before their arrival."

"You were certainly sure of your acceptance, sir," Abby said stiffly.

"No, Abby, my love, only hopeful. But what I feel for you is so overwhelming, I could not accept that it was one-sided. And even if you only accepted my offer because you do not want to be on the shelf, I promise I will do all that is within my power to make you happy."

The sincerity of his words melted Abby's indignation. "Oh, Giles, I love you with all my heart. I owe you so much for making it possible for my sisters to marry for love, but it compares little with the love that fills my heart when I even think about you. I hoped for happiness for my sisters. I have been granted that. But you have given me the greatest gift of all, my very own love."

With her heart throbbing against his, Mr. Russell said as he lowered his lips to hers, "I believe we should be married first, my love, since you are the eldest. For I fear I cannot wait very long before claiming you as my wife."

"An excellent suggestion, Giles, and we can serve lemon cake at our reception, so that others may find happiness like ours," Abby teased.

"Who needs lemon cake when the most beautiful girl in the world is in my arms?" Giles asked before demonstrating his point most ably.

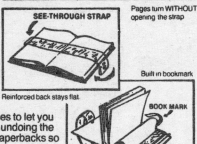